# The
# Wizard's
# Grandson

by

## Levi Samuel

The Wizard's Grandson
Eldarlands Publishing
Copyright © 2021

Story and Cover Art by Levi Samuel.

Genre: Urban Fantasy / Witches and Wizards

First Edition

ISBN 13: 978-1-950541-14-0

I'd like to dedicate this book to my grandpa,
James "Shorty" Rikard.
Rest well, Grandpa.

Thank you so much for your interest in this book. Your support is what allows me to do what I love. Please take a few minutes to leave a review. They help us more than you know.

Additionally, if you'd like exclusive access to a free book, or to stay up to date with my latest projects, consider subscribing to my newsletter at, http://eepurl.com/dxRUvL

Levi Samuel

December 2021

# Contents

# Chapter 1
## Eavesdropping

The thumping tick of an old analogue clock echoed in my head, drumming away the seconds. I wish I could say I'd been paying some kind of attention to my surroundings, but I can't. I was too excited.

It was the last day of school, the last day before summer vacation, and most important of all, it was the end of my childhood.

Yep! Today is my thirteenth birthday. I'd been waiting for this day since I was old enough to understand the concept of time. The big one-three. I had the whole summer ahead of me. Next year I'd be a wholly new person, teeming with experiences and life lessons unknown to the lowly twelve-year-olds.

Being the last of my friends to finally reach this milestone, I was excited to have finally caught up. Though one final obstacle remained before me. Before I could properly ring in my birthday with a massive party to dominate all other parties, I had to go visit my grandpa.

The school's obnoxious bell sounded from the intercom, jolting me from my daydream.

"Earth to A-A-Ron!" Raj yelled an inch from my ear.

"What?" I spun to face him, seeing that mischievous smile permanently etched on his thin brown lips.

Raj had been my best friend since kindergarten. Back then he couldn't speak so clear and I guess he had trouble pronouncing my name. I don't know why he continuously calls me 'A-A-Ron', but he's the only one allowed to do so. I'm not a violent person but anyone else would get a knuckle sandwich.

"Finally! I've only been trying to get your attention for the last five minutes."

"You have it now. What do you want?" Raj was notorious for making grand exaggerations. Just last week I made the mistake of being the first to fall asleep when I stayed the night at his house. When he pushed me off the top bunk he swears I floated to the floor, but speaking as the one who woke up on the floor, I'm pretty sure we both know what really happened.

I grabbed my backpack and began stuffing my books atop several already crumpled pieces of paper that had gathered in the bottom.

"What time do you want me to come over? Oh, and how many people will be there? My mom is ordering us pizza."

We made for the door, joining the ever-growing sea of people filling the halls. The place was packed with kids struggling to escape. Locker doors were abandoned, many of them still open and displaying whatever trash had been left behind. A great deal was scattered about the floor, stomped into submission by hundreds of uncaring students, each one fighting toward the exit. That was one thing I could say about my generation. We weren't the most courteous of sorts.

Raj walked beside me. He'd been talking the entire time though truth be told I hadn't been listening. Out of nowhere his voice reached me across the roar of chatter.

"Mags says she has a big game planned but she doesn't want a big group."

"What'd I say?" A tall girl with pale skin and freckles fell in beside us. Mags was the first in our class to hit teenager status. She was already fourteen and several inches taller than me. Black streaks interrupted her sea of wavy red hair. She wore torn overalls stained with paint and an oversized flannel shirt over the top like a jacket.

"Raj was saying you don't want a large group for tonight's game."

"He's right. Do you know how many are coming?"

I shrugged. I'd only invited a handful of people but I had no idea who was planning to show. Raj and Mags were obvious. We'd only been talking about the big event for a month now, pretty much ever since Raj's birthday. The truth was, I didn't really like anyone else. The sporty kids were good to get in with if you wanted to be popular, which I didn't. And the smart kids were bullied by pretty much everyone. Then you had groups like ours. We were neither involved in extracurriculars or considered overly smart, despite fair grades. We simply wanted to get by without too much attention.

"I'll plan for five. More than that and I can't promise a TPK."

"Good luck." Raj challenged. "My rogue maxed on stealth last game. You'll need a nat-twenty to even find me."

I wasn't sure if it was sunlight hitting us as we passed through the front doors or something else but I saw the fire in Mags' eyes. A smirk came to my lips.

"Do you really want to test me?"

"I—um—no." Raj lowered his head in defeat. It was an unofficial rule not to challenge the GM. That was a surefire way to get your character killed.

We reached the bike rack and I quickly twisted the dials on my chain lock and stowed it in the side pocket of my backpack. Straddling the seat, I waited for them to get their bikes free.

"So what's the plan?" Raj prompted as if he'd asked several times already.

"I guess be at my house around five. I should be home by then. I have to go see my grandpa before I can do anything."

"That sucks." Raj added.

"Whatever! I wish I could still go see *my* grandpa." Mags retorted. "I'll see you guys in a few hours."

I watched her ride away, disappearing in the mass of students headed for the car line.

"When are you gonna tell her?" Raj asked, failing to hide his smile.

"Tell her what?"

"Duh. That you like her."

"Who says I do? She's cool but we're just friends."

"So says you. I know you have a crush on her. You always smile when she's around. And you never give her crap like you do me."

"Maybe that's because she doesn't pull stupid pranks on me all the time." It sounded harsher than I'd meant but Raj proved my point almost immediately.

I tried to place my feet on the pedals only to have them snag. I tripped and nearly fell over, catching my bike on the way down.

Raucous laugher bellowed from Raj as if he'd just witnessed the funniest thing ever.

I glared at him and looked down, finding my shoelaces tied together. I have no clue how he'd managed it but that's the thing about Raj; he's always doing stuff like that.

"Maybe if you paid a little more attention I wouldn't be able to get so much over on you." His laughter slowly faded away, as if every memory brough it back in a slightly weaker form. Finally, he sighed and turned to watch the busses leave.

"You just wait. One of these days I'm going to pay you back for all the pranks you've played on me." I fixed my shoes and repositioned the seat.

I wish I'd been quick-witted enough to prank him before he returned to his senses. As it were, I wasn't. I didn't even know how I'd get him back. He lived for pranks. On more than one occasion he'd reminded me that a good rogue was prepared for anything. I couldn't fault him there but I failed to see how expired fireworks or a sock full of dryer lint would come in handy during daily life. Sadly, those were just a few examples of the items occupying his backpack.

"It'll be a cold day before you get one over on me!" Raj taunted, jerking the string of a party popper he'd somehow materialized.

Confetti exploded in my face and his laughter returned, though less genuine than before.

Shaking my head, I mounted my bike a second time and started down the sidewalk that ran the length of the school.

Raj caught up and we rode together for the first several blocks. It was a familiar path; down the alley, around the back side of the football field, and into the new subdivision just behind the school. In no time we were off school property.

Raj left me once we reached the other side and headed toward his home a few blocks away.

I continued forward, across the undeveloped field. It was a bit of a rough ride. The ground was uneven and waist high grass swayed in the afternoon breeze. I followed the narrow trail I'd ridden so many times before. I'm not sure what created it but it had been here as long as I could remember.

I pedaled my way toward the thick patch of trees at the center of the field. Some might have called it a small forest but I wouldn't know. Not yet anyway. Today of all days was the day I planned to change that.

The sun was on the descent, making that orange haze it often cast in late summer, but it was still plenty bright.

I rode hard, my front tire aimed for the narrow path through the trees. I was just about to cross the threshold into the unknown when I slammed on my brakes and slid to a stop, the same as I'd done every week for as long as I can recall. At that moment I was fairly certain, unless something drastic happened between now and then, I'd do it again next week.

I wish I could explain my fear of the forest. Logically, there was no reason to be afraid. I could see straight through to the other side. The path was fairly straight and nothing looked out of the ordinary. Despite all that, I'd never been able to bring myself to step inside. A foreboding dread set in every time I even got near it.

I stared headlong into the shadows of the forest path cut through the scariest patch of woods in the world. I couldn't move.

Drawing a deep breath, trying to calm the beating in my chest, I wiped the sweat from my forehead and watched it soak into my shirt sleeve. It was one of those weird times of year where it was cold in the morning and hot in the afternoon. Strange for the time of year but the weather patterns seemed to be off by about three months ever since the ice storm when I was a kid. How else do you explain snow storms in May or 90-degree temperatures in November?

I couldn't help but recall the haiku my mom had made a habit of saying, especially when commenting on my clothing choices. She'd say I could add as many layers as I wanted but I could only remove so many. I'd learned it was sometimes easier to simply agree with her and be on my way.

The extra layers clinging to my skin felt constricting. I wanted out of them almost as much as I wanted away from the forest path that had tormented me for so long.

All my life I'd been made to visit my grandfather. When I was a kid my parents would bring me in the car. It was a longer distance but didn't take near as much time. Then, when I was ten, I started walking home from school. My mom decided if I was old enough to walk home, I was old enough to visit my grandpa by myself. It wasn't long after that when I got my bike and was expected to visit him every week— every week for the rest of my life.

The weekly trip had been cramping my style for quite some time now. It's not that I don't like my grandpa. In fact, as far as grandpas go, he's probably pretty average, though I have no basis for comparison. It's simply that visiting him cuts into the time that I could be doing other more important stuff. And if I'm being honest, I've always found him a bit strange; like he's testing me for something I'm supposed to know but never do. For instance, the ability to be on time by crossing the forest path, which I constantly fail.

Honestly, I don't know what the problem is. The forest just feels wrong. The tree limbs reach out like wispy fingers, waiting to grab me. Strange noises echo in the shadows. Movement passes out the corner of my eye but when I look nothing's there. I can't put it into words but it makes me feel uneasy. I start to sweat, even if I'm cold. My heart starts to race. My brain tells me to run far away and never return.

And yet, each week I return trying to work up the courage to race through and cut my time in half.

I glanced at my watch and silently cursed myself. I'd already lost fifteen minutes to this attempt and hadn't managed to take a single step forward.

Lowering my head in defeat, I lifted my bike and turned left to begin the long ride of shame around the forest's edge. It was still shorter than taking the road but not by much.

The early afternoon sun was nearly blinding by the time I returned to the world of paved roads and concrete sidewalks. A few minutes after that I reached my destination.

The large parking lot always seemed empty save for a few cars that changed places on occasion. The sign out front read *Shad E Acres Retirement Home.*

I always found the name strange, like a typo to what should have been a common enough name. Everyone called it Shady Acres anyway.

Truth be told, I'd never been able to understand why my grandpa chose to stayed in such a place. It was boring. There were several bricked buildings, all single story with the exception of an old clock tower along the far back row.

Not much else could be seen beyond the stone wall that wrapped the property. It felt like an impenetrable barrier, only accessible through the single gate at the head of the parking lot.

I'd been here enough to know everything even without seeing it. There were several concrete walkways that led everywhere. Perfect grass filled the areas between walkways and courts. It remained green year-round despite weather. My father claimed it was fake but I didn't understand why anyone would bother with fake grass.

Beyond the wall reminded me of the playground at school; that is if the playground was much larger and had more than one basketball court and a few benches. This place had a swimming pool with two diving boards and numerous courts for just about every game I knew about. It even had a small golf course that people sometimes played.

I was slightly disgruntled that I'd never been allowed to drive the carts.

Even when people were out the place always felt empty, like they were there for show and nothing else. None of the people had ever talked to me or even looked my direction. If not for my ability to see them they may as well have not existed at all.

In fact, the only people who ever paid me any attention were the staff and my grandpa. It made me wonder what it would be like to live here, but I was fairly certain I didn't want to find out.

I approached the guard shack and slipped the front wheel of my bike into the rack. Pressing the black button on the front of the metal box, a static voice echoed from the speaker.

"Welcome back to Shady Acres. Come on in Aaron."

I was always surprised when the disembodied voice knew my name. I should have been used to it by now. They always knew who I was and I didn't have the slightest clue who they were.

The metal gate buzzed and began to open of its own accord. I carefully stepped through and started down the walkway. The echo of my shoes on concrete was interrupted by the clank of the gate behind me.

In no time I was at the front entrance, a set of gray painted doors that eerily reminded me of the doors at school.

Inside I was greeted by the familiar plain white walls of the lobby. I suppose there's only so much you can do with painted cinderblock. It made decoration difficult beyond that of an elementary school classroom.

The room was wide and narrow with a single wooden door to the right. There were blue cushioned chairs against the wall to the left of the entrance, and across the way a large glass window showed another smaller room with a door on its back wall.

The receptionist offered a smile through the glass. He looked slightly older than my dad and wore a strange white shirt that looked more like a bath robe by design. I guessed it was the uniform here. I'd seen the same shirt in different colors on every employee I'd met.

His voice reached me through the circular hole in the glass. It felt warm and welcoming. "Good afternoon, Aaron. Giles is on his way down. Feel free to wait in the lounge."

"Thank you." It felt weird hearing him called *Giles*. He was Grandpa. He had no other names.

I turned and pulled open the wooden door. It led into a hallway that continued left, along the outside of the receptionist office. Instead of following the hall I went straight across and through another wooden door, this one with a small rectangular window above the knob.

The lounge was a large room that was twice as long as it was wide. An old wooden table sat in the center with four wooden chairs tucked along both long sides and one at each end. The backrests were ancient and extravagant and a plump needle-worked cushion rested in each seat, offering support from the wooden frame.

According to my grandpa, both the table and chairs were handmade by the residence but I couldn't imagine how anyone could build such a thing without machinery.

The far narrow wall had an old box style TV surrounded by empty leather recliners. It was playing some old black and white western where the gunshots were nothing but excessive smoke and people rolled when they were hit but never actually died.

A smaller round table sat in front of a pair of windows to my right. It had four plastic folding chairs tucked around it with a partially completed puzzle scattered across the top.

Shelves of old board games and magazines and books rested here and there and a tack board hung on the wall between the two entry doors that had an *Arts and Crafts Winner* announcement but it didn't give any information as far as I could tell.

Despite the signs of activity, I wasn't surprised the room was vacant. It was always like this. In fact, I can't remember ever seeing anyone other than Grandpa during my numerous visits.

Turning my attention to the long banquet table that ran the back wall, I was starting to feel hungry. It had been a few hours since my last meal and the various treats, snack platters, and candy were tempting me.

I approached the table and helped myself to a few bite sized candy bars and a small paper plate of trail mix, crackers, cheese, and salami.

Without another thought, I made my way to the central table and took my usual seat. I'd narrowly finished my first mini sandwich when I heard the door open. I glanced up to find my grandpa walking toward me.

He looked the same as always with his long gray hair and wrinkled skin. He was slightly more plump than most people his age, though truth be told I wasn't sure how old he was. He'd pretty much always looked this way, wearing his crescent shaped glasses and red suspenders over a perfectly pressed shirt that was habitually tucked in. He also always wore either beige or gray pants and brown leather shoes.

If not for the alternating colors between pants and shirts I would have imagined him wearing the same clothes every day his entire life. There was only one detail that shattered his otherwise perfect old man persona. He wore golden earrings that were shaped like some kind of bird.

"I hear someone has a birthday coming up." Grandpa said, approaching the table.

"Yeah. Today actually."

Grandpa pulled the chair on the end and plopped down with a grunt. "I'll tell ya, kiddo, these old bones aren't what they once were." He rubbed his knee briefly before staring up at me with a smile. "So, tell me about it. Big plans? Your mother tells me it's the big one-three."

"I have a few friends coming over. It's no big deal." I lied. It was in fact a huge deal. I just didn't want to tell him that. He might want to show up or something and I wasn't sure if I was ready for my friends to meet the weird old man I was forced to spend time with every week. Fearing my true intentions were showing, I stuffed a cracker sandwich into my mouth and began to chew.

"I remember my thirteenth. It was a night I'll never forget. That reminds me. I got you a birthday present."

I'm not entirely sure how the wrapped box ended up on the table in front of him. He hadn't had it when he walked in. I'm certain I would have seen it. Yet here it was, resting between us. The gold foil paper and hand wrapped bow made all kinds of a spectacle in the reflected overhead lights.

"Your celebration of birth isn't official for another few hours but I trust you can keep this between us? Your mother would kill me if she knew I gave it to you early."

I have to admit I was curious. I'd had my eye on a new gaming console for a while now and the box was about the perfect size. If my guess was right my grandpa might have just climbed from the lamest to the coolest in one shot.

Hiding my excitement, I pulled the gift toward me and sized it up. It was heavy. That was a good sign, though it felt more solid than I would have imagined. Swallowing hard, I managed to speak through the last bits of cracker and cheese clinging to the roof of my mouth. "Can I open it now?"

"I'll make you a deal. If you can beat me in a game of chess, I'll let you open it. If not, you'll have to wait until tonight."

I couldn't stop the sigh from escaping. There was no way I was going to beat him. Even if I understood the game beyond how each piece moved there was no hope. Ever since I was little he'd used the game as a means of settling disputes. Who does the dishes? A game of chess. Who mows the lawn? A game of chess. He even challenged me once about who was going to throw his smelly socks in the hamper. Needless to say, it was a lost cause. Still, I knew I wasn't going to be able to escape without seeing it to the end.

He had the board set up and ready before I'd even had a chance to answer. And within the first four rounds it was over. I'm not sure how it happened but I found myself in check before I could hope to form a strategy. He usually gave the illusion I was doing good but this time he beat me ruthlessly without an ounce of reserve.

"Well played, Grandpa." I scooted my chair and got to my feet. "I need to get going. Mom wants me to do the dishes and take out the trash before she gets home from work."

Grandpa nodded and slid the present closer toward the edge of the table. "A deal's a deal. You can open it before you leave."

"Um—You won fair and square." I corrected, surprised by his gesture.

"You sure?" He asked, his gaze locked firmly on me. The hint of a smile peeked around the edges.

"Pretty sur—" I paused, staring at the board once again. He'd never announced checkmate or even check for that matter but I couldn't see any way out of the position he'd left me in. My king was thoroughly trapped with a straight line to his queen and nowhere to run, much less block. It was then I realized it was my turn and I had him in the exact trap he'd used on me. "Wha— how? Um—Checkmate?" I moved my queen one square to the left, shielding my king and placing his in imminent danger. What was better, his own pieces had him pinned with nowhere to go and nothing capable of blocking. It was my first ever victory and I wouldn't have known if he hadn't pointed it out.

I heaved the present and gave it a firm shake, listening for loose parts. I didn't hear any.

"Go on then, open it."

I started to inspect the paper for a seam when the door opened and I found myself staring at a rather tall man with dark skin and curly gray hair.

He wore a deep red cardigan and thick glasses over his bloodshot eyes. Considering this was the visitor's lounge I shouldn't have been surprised but this was the first time I'd seen anyone except Grandpa in here. A part of me believed he was the only resident.

"I'm not interrupting anything am I?" The old man asked, seemingly as surprised to find us as I was him.

"Not at all, Grigori. I'd like you to meet my grandson, Aaron." Grandpa gestured the old man over.

I hadn't noticed how frail he looked at a distance yet there was a strength in his eyes I hadn't seen elsewhere.

"Nice to meet ya, son." Grigori scanned the chessboard and looked up in surprise. "Did you do this?"

"Ye—Yes, sir."

"I'll be. I've never seen anyone beat this old coot. You're somethin' special, kid."

I was beginning to get embarrassed. I wasn't much for praise of any kind. What was weird though, there was something about the old man I didn't trust. I wanted to open my present but something told me it was a mistake to do so with this stranger present. Something about him didn't feel right. "Thanks. Anyway, I've got to run. I'll see you next week, Grandpa."

Grabbing my backpack from beneath the table I stuffed the foil wrapped box inside. I was surprised it fit. I figured I'd have to leave it unzipped during the ride home but it seemed as if the two were made for each other.

"Aaron, hold on a moment. I'll be—"

I was off and out the door before Grandpa could finished his sentence.

I'm not entirely sure if I paused before or after I'd heard my name but I found myself in the hall pressed against the door listening to their conversation.

"So that's the kid, huh? Does he know?"

"It is. And not yet." Grandpa responded.

"He's close. I can feel it."

"Let him be a kid. He deserves that much."

"Can't change what's already set in motion. You aren't doing him any favors by waiting. The more he knows the better off he'll be."

"I know. I just can't help but feel like it's too soon."

"None of us had a choice. It's going to happen one way or another. Coddling will only hurt him in the long run."

Hearing footsteps down the hall, I spun and pressed my way through the other door into the lobby. I was outside and running to my bike before I knew what was happening. All I could think about was their conversation. I wasn't sure what they were talking about but whatever it was I didn't like the sound of it.

The Wizard's Grandson

Levi Samuel

# Chapter 2
## An Unexpected Surprise

When I made it back to my bike I may as well have been in a different world.

On the surface nothing had changed. The retirement home's parking lot was still just as empty as ever. The sun had only fallen marginally since I'd gone inside.

Truth be told, I don't know why it felt so different but I couldn't shake the feeling I was being followed. Every hair on my body stood on end. I could almost see the steam from my breath but it wasn't cold enough for that. Even the fading sunlight, despite its orange glow that stretched across everything, cast ominous heavy shadows.

My heart pounded in my chest as anxiety grew. A quick glance at the clock tower on the far side of the grounds told me I had about thirty minutes to get home. My gut told me I had less than that.

In near panic I ripped my bike from the rack and jumped on at a run. I felt like I was in one of those movies where the people are running for safety down a long hallway and the lights are systematically going dark overhead. I was at the edge of illumination, peddling as hard and as fast as I could with shadows quickly gaining on me.

I couldn't risk looking behind. I knew if I did whatever was there would get me. All I could do was keep moving forward— keep fleeing as fast as possible.

In no time I was in desperate need of air. I raced across the street, toward the familiar and intimidating patch of trees. I couldn't go in. Whatever was in there was worse than whatever was behind me.

My tires tore through the grass and dirt as I slid and hooked the bike around to shoot down the narrow path on the outskirts.

Some might say I was just being paranoid. Or maybe that I was that kid afraid of his own shadow. I don't think the description accurately applies. I wasn't always like this. In fact, these kinds of things only started happening recently.

Over the last few months I'd started seeing things that weren't there. I'd see shadows in places where none existed. I'd feel the icy breath of death upon my neck. Things moved at the edge of my vision, disappearing when I turned to look. What had me most worried was how frequent it was becoming.

It'd gone from maybe once a week to nearly every day, until days like today where it was happening almost constant.

I'd considered maybe the events of our game was playing tricks on my mind but there was nothing logical about such an assumption.

When Mags took over as game master she decided to do a horror storyline. Last week we'd stumbled upon an old crypt.

Raj had failed his detect traps roll and inadvertently awoken a nightmare creature. We barely escaped with our lives.

I'd used every resource I had at my disposal and still only made it out with four hit points to spare.

Poor Raj had had to make three constitution rolls before he finally stabilized.

I didn't know if it was the adrenaline of the game blending into real life or something more sinister but I was starting to think I was haunted.

Whatever was following me now felt more malicious than a simple haunting. I don't know how to explain it but I could feel that whatever it was, it was big and it was dangerous.

I also felt it was somehow tied to the conversation I'd overheard minutes before. I couldn't shake the feeling everyone knew something I did not.

My legs felt as if they might fall off. Finally, I reached the far side of the field. I darted through the subdivision where I'd left Raj maybe an hour earlier and hopped the curb into the park that rested just outside my subdivision.

As if I'd passed through some kind of protective barrier, I immediately felt better. I felt safe, like whatever had been chasing me was suddenly gone.

I came to a gradual stop and turned to look, hoping for some assurance I wasn't simply going crazy, not that the sight of some monster would help with that diagnosis.

I was both relieved and a little disappointed that nothing was there. I was alone at the edge of a park with the fading sun and the distant houses to comfort me.

Taking a moment to catch my breath and let my heart calm, I dismounted my bike and started walking across the park. For all I knew the chase would resume when I reached the far side. I wanted to be ready if that was the case.

The park was eerily quiet. The swings squeaked as they slowly drifted in the light breeze. The merry-go-round sat stationary with its woodchip filled foot path around the outer edge. The polished metal slide reflected the sun, sending up heat waves that would likely cook anyone who used it.

Being a Friday evening, I would have thought at least someone would have been at the park. Fremont Hills was a small town and most people, especially those with younger kids, visited on the weekends. It was my opinion Friday evening was just as much a part of the weekend as Saturday. It seemed a strange occurrence no one was around and I couldn't help but think of a ghost town that hadn't seen life in forever.

I lived in an upscale neighborhood on the western edge of town. It wasn't an overly large town by any means, but it had everything I thought a town needed.

There was plenty of housing, which seemed to be the only thing it had when we moved in. The school was next to come. Before, I'd spent kindergarten at Ridge Lawn Elementary. That's where I met Raj.

Over the past couple years they'd built a number of restaurants and stores in the hopes of breathing life into town but I felt it just muddied traffic. We used to have to go to one of the two surrounding cities for everything. In some ways it felt like we were that dividing line between two rivalries.

Even at my age, we were constantly being forced to pick who to support when any major event happened between the surrounding cities. In fact, the only time my parents seemed to argue was when their opinions on such events differed.

And of course when it came to sporting events we were considered the black sheep, competing with both equally and hated just the same. That was part of the reason I refrained from participating. I didn't care for such rivalries and I didn't see any reason to get involved.

Reaching the park's edge I mounted my bike and prepared for the worst. To my relief nothing came charging into the open. I was in the clear. I crossed the street into my subdivision and started home.

Turning onto my street, I scanned the half block to my house. To my surprise both my parents' cars were parked in the driveway. I didn't know exactly how long it had taken me to get home but there was no way they should have beaten me. If this were any other day I would have had the house to myself for at least another hour before they came home.

That left two possibilities. Either they hadn't gone to work, or they were home super early. For that to happen, today of all days, I could only imagine one reason. They were throwing me a surprise party.

That was the logical explanation. Why else would my mom have insisted I visit my grandpa on my birthday? And with all the questions Raj had been asking at school, I should have known something was up. They needed to keep me out of the house to make the preparations.

I started up the slight incline of the drive. Just behind my mom's car I swung my leg over the bike seat and stepped off. There was a narrow path between the bush shrouded fence to my right and their cars to my left, which I navigated past and approached the side of the garage where I parked my bike. Strangely, Raj and Mags' bikes were nowhere to be seen.

If my estimates were correct, it was only slightly earlier than I'd told them. With the obvious surprise party in the works, they should have arrived by now. Of course, they could have been dropped off by their parents and were inside, hiding in wait. That had to be it.

Playing along, I made my way around the nose of my dad's car and onto the stone walkway that led to the front porch. Making as much noise as possible, I jingled my sparse key collection as I located the correct one. If they were planning to surprise me I wanted to let them know I was home. Afterall, a surprise wasn't any fun if they didn't know I was coming.

The door wasn't locked which caught me off guard. I twisted the knob and pushed it open.

Stepping inside, my entry was met with silence. I waited at the foyer expecting to hear shouts of 'Surprise!', but none came.

The living room to my right was empty save for the central couch, coffee and end tables, lamps, and a few decorations my mom was overly protective of. The TV was off and sparse sunlight drifted across the room through the thin curtains covering the windows.

The dining room table to my left was unadorned and the wooden chairs were tucked neatly beneath. The chandelier hanging over its center was off, though the polished metal and glass sparkled reflected light on the walls. No sound came from the kitchen entrance beyond.

My thoughts of a surprise party were rapidly evaporating in the silence. Still, my parents' cars were here. That meant they had to be as well.

As if in answer to my question I heard voices up the stairs and to the left of the mezzanine near my parents' bedroom.

I closed the front door and hurriedly skipped up the hardwood steps just across the entryway. I reached the top to the open balcony and rounded the polished banister. With each step I felt the carpet absorb my weight as I approached their room. The door was pushed to but not sealed. I could hear my mom talking just inside.

"Hello? Mom, Dad?" I pushed the door open a little, finding my mom standing over a suitcase. It was sprawled out across the bed and half full of plastic wrapped clothing.

She was in the middle of folding another article when she looked up and smiled at me. "Oh, hey, honey. How was school?"

It felt more like a customary greeting than an actual inquiry.

"Um—fine." Something wasn't right. It was my birthday. They should have been preparing for my party, not packing their bags.

My dad appeared at the entrance to their walk-in closet. He held two similar colored suits, as if he couldn't decide which was better. "Oh, hey, Aaron. How was school?"

"What's going on?"

"Your mother and I have a flight to catch. She has a seminar first thing in the morning. I'm sure we told you."

"Um—No. Nobody said anything about a seminar. What about my birthday?" I wish I could have taken some pleasure in their momentary oversight but I couldn't. I was aghast. How could they have forgotten about me?

"Honey, your birthday is—" My mom trailed off, seeming to have come to the realization that she'd made a huge mistake. "Um—Well, we'll only be gone for a couple days. When we get back we'll throw you a proper party. Right, Hun?"

She batted at my dad, drawing his attention from the monumental decision of which suit to pack.

"What? Oh—uh—right."

"Unbelievable!" I spun on my heel and rushed off toward my room. I could hear my mom shouting after me but I wasn't sure what she'd said. It wasn't until my door had slammed and I'd fallen face first onto my bed that I heard her footsteps behind me.

"Aaron, I won't tolerate that attitude!" She proclaimed outside my door. I was glad she didn't just barge in though I knew it wasn't beneath her. "If you want to have some friends over, that's fine. Just try to keep it contained."

Her words fueled the fire burning within me. My friends had already made the arrangements to come over. This simply confirmed she'd forgotten all about my party. Growling my anger, I pushed myself off the bed and marched toward the door, stomping for effect. I reached out and twisted the knob, ripping it toward me. "They're already coming over. Unlike you they didn't forget about my birthday!"

I tried to slam the door to make my point but she caught it before I could get it latched.

"Young man, your father and I have to attend this seminar. We don't have a choice in the matter. You need to remember you don't pay the bills here. Until you do, I expect a little more respect!" She glared, daring me to say anything to the contrary.

"Yes, ma'am." I squeaked, though I wasn't happy about it.

"Good. Now, your grandfather is coming to keep an eye on you. I expect you to be on your best behavior. Like I said, you can have some friends over, but try to keep it contained. Now, if you'll excuse me I have to finish packing." She turned and was gone before I could add anything, not that I had anything to add.

Sighing, I pushed the door closed and turned back to my room.

All things considered it wasn't as messy as it usually was. I only had a few articles of dirty clothes lying on the floor. And most of the trash was in the small trash bin beside my desk. It probably would have all been in there if the bin weren't already full. I had a few small posters tacked to the wall, foldouts of some old gaming magazines I'd found. I had some pictures of various monsters or cool looking spell sigils I'd drawn.

The biggest piece of furniture I had, other than my bed or dresser was my bookshelf. It was nearly overflowing. The middle and bottom shelves were completely full of gaming books. And the top shelf was packed two deep with various fantasy novels I'd come across. Most I'd managed to read but some I had trouble getting through. It wasn't so much the writing as much as it was the silly decisions most of the characters made.

As I returned to my bed I grabbed my backpack from the floor where I'd dropped it. This wasn't anywhere close to how I'd expected my night to go.

I plopped onto the springy mattress and opened my bag. The present Grandpa had given me took up most of the space. Its foil wrap and bow glittered in the artificial light. I couldn't help but think that if my suspicions of what it contained were correct, maybe my birthday might be salvageable.

I carefully retrieved the package and placed it on the bed beside me. I hadn't noticed prior but there were no seams or folds or tape as far as I could tell, just the single obtuse ribbon resting at the top center. It had long curly tails that danced chaotically under the slightest movement and bands that stretched around and hugged tight to all four corners.

I inspected the package carefully, unsure how I was going to open it. I could rip the paper of course but that seemed so brutish. I'd given up tearing paper a long time ago, settling rather on careful peeling of tape and removing it in a single sheet like a reverse puzzle.

Unfortunately, my dad would immediately wad it into a ball and throw it in a trash bag which always irritated me. It was an uncontrollable compulsion that I had yet to defeat and I suspected he did it because he knew it annoyed me.

This present was proving to be my biggest obstacle yet, pristine paper that encompassed like a rectangle shaped eggshell.

I ran my fingers along the edges, feeling for any hidden differences. The top, bottom, and left sides were firm as could be. The other three had a little give before they became equally firm. I had no idea what was inside but my hopes of finding a new console were rapidly deteriorating.

"How do I open you?" I asked aloud, not expecting an answer. There had to be a seam somewhere. How else had Grandpa wrapped it? It wasn't like he could simply place the present inside and shrink it to fit. Even if he had there should still be an opening—somewhere.

On a whim, I tugged at one of the ribbon's tails. It unraveled into a heap of loose sparkly lace and no sooner than the corners fell free the sides of the wrapping unfolded to reveal a rather large book draped in golden foil.

On one hand my last shred of hope evaporated. On the other, I felt a strange pull toward the book. It intrigued me in a way I'd never felt before. It was almost like the promised of secrets that only I was destined to learn.

Removing the now loose golden paper, I inspected the thick tome. I couldn't make sense of what I was seeing. Its size alone was baffling. It seemed to have grown since being unwrapped. There was no way it could have fit inside my backpack.

The thing had to be at least four inches thick with dense yellow pages and it was easily as wide as my forearm was long, and as tall as my leg from knee to hip. It was the largest book I'd ever seen. Not even my math book was so large and it had all kinds of useless information in it.

Folding the foil paper, I tossed it aside and studied the ancient leather wrapped cover. There was no telling how old it was or what it was about. It was daunting to gaze upon but felt somehow familiar, like an old friend I hadn't seen in a long time.

There were strange depictions carved into the surface which reminded me of some of the spell sigils I had posted about the room. These felt more mysterious though. Most of mine were just things I saw in my head or found in some of my gaming books. The ones on this book felt more real.

I couldn't help but wonder why my grandpa had given it to me. Moreover, where he'd even found such a thing.

I ran my fingers across the markings that I assumed were the title. I had no idea what it said. It was written in some strange language but I felt it was probably Latin. Afterall, what else would some mysterious tome be titled with?

Of all the questions that poured through my mind, only one answer came to me. This had to be some long-forgotten spell compendium to a game I'd never heard about.

Fortunately, I was good at retrofitting outdated PHBs. If this book had anything of use I was sure I could have it fully updated and ready for modern gameplay within a couple of days.

The doorbell rang and I heard my mom's footsteps rush downstairs. I could always tell the difference. She was lighter and faster, whereas my dad took his time. I got the feeling he didn't care if whoever was at the door waited or not.

"Hello, Raj. Yes. He's in his room. Feel free to head on up."

I listened to the footsteps hurry upstairs and approach my door. There was a light knock and almost immediately it creaked open.

I rolled to my side and glanced through the crack to find Raj staring at me. His short dark hair blended with his caramel colored skin in the shadows, leaving only his disembodied eyes visible in the opening.

I broke my gaze on him and glanced to the alarm clock on my nightstand. It was just after five. I hadn't done much of anything to get ready for my nonparty.

Turning back to Raj, I waved him in. "Don't just stand there looking at me all creepy like. Come in."

It made no sense why he'd opened the door but gone no further, though knowing him he was probably arranging a bucket of water to fall on me, or setting up some other nefarious prank to which I'd fall victim.

He opened the door fully but didn't enter. "I was waiting for an invitation."

"So you opened my door and stared in, but decided to wait for an invite?"

"Yes? Was that not already clear?"

A heavy sigh escaped me. It was times like these I was happy to be an only child.

Forcing as much sarcasm as I could muster, I waved him forward. "Won't you please do me the favor of entering my domain?"

Raj charged in and abandoning reserve, belly flopped on the bed beside me.

The surface bounced hard, sending both myself and the book into the air. When we landed, the book fell open to a page near the center.

I had no idea what I was looking at but I couldn't look away. Somewhere in the distance I thought I heard my mom yell to stop jumping on the bed but it may as well have been spoken to someone else.

"What's that?" Raj asked, leaning to get a closer look.

"I don't know. My grandpa gave it to me. I think it's some early edition spell book but I can't read the name."

"Cool!"

Together we stared at the page, lost in its numerous faded lines sprawled into the most intricate sigil I'd ever seen. Whoever'd done the artwork was amazingly precise. Each line was crisp and clear, and tiny scrollwork had been inked into the spaces between lines.

Finally breaking away from the image, unsure how long I'd been trapped within, I closed the book and turned to Raj. "So, my parents forgot about my birthday."

"No way!"

"Way. They're headed to some conference halfway across the country. They called my grandpa to come babysit me. As if sending me to see him earlier wasn't enough."

"That sucks!"

"I know. And to make matters worse, they act like it's my fault. Like I'm supposed to remind them when my birthday is. I'm pretty sure they're supposed to keep track of that kind of stuff."

"Maybe they're trying to make you think they forgot so they can surprise you with something big later?"

"I doubt it. They seem pretty set on leaving. They've been packing since before I got home."

"What about game?"

"I don't know. I guess it doesn't change much. I was just hoping to have a little more party type stuff beforehand. Now, it feels like just another normal game night. That's not how I imagined my thirteenth birthday would go."

"I know what you mean. When my Upanayana happened last month, it was nothing like how I'd expected it."

"That's the thing. You still had a whole celebration to mark your coming of age. I'm not even getting that. My parents are leaving. Like my birthday is just another day to them."

"We could always do something different."

"Like what?"

"We could go to that new ice cream parlor in the strip mall. No adults. No responsibilities. Just us roaming the town and doing all the things we've talked about but never actually taken the time to do."

"What about my grandpa? I'm pretty sure he'd notice our absence."

"A-A-Ron, my friend." Raj paused, shaking his head. He crawled off the bed and got to his feet. "What do old people do?"

"Go to work and pay bills?"

"That's what our parents do. What do really old people do?"

"Sit around eating snacks and talking about 'the good ole days'." I rocked my arms for emphasis.

"And after that?" Raj leaned in as if he were hinting at something.

"They— fall asleep?"

"Exactly! We just have to wait for him to fall asleep."

I wasn't a fan of most of Raj's schemes. He was always making these elaborate plans, detailing each and every scenario we were likely to encounter, all the while waiting for the perfect moment to enact any one of them. Most of the time he spent so much time planning and waiting for the perfect moment that he rarely got the chance to actually use any of them.

I figured this was one of those moments. He'd probably either forget all about it by the time my grandpa arrived, or take so long to make happen that we'd miss the opportunity altogether.

As if my thoughts triggered it the doorbell rang and I heard my mom answer.

"Hey Dad. Thanks for coming."

"It's my pleasure. Where's the birthday boy?"

"He's upstairs. I'll let him know you've arrived."

I stared at Raj, allowing my annoyance to show. It seemed my night of hell was about to begin.

# Chapter 3
## Pranks and Presents

Holding the thick curtain aside I peered out my bedroom window, watching in desperation as my parents loaded into my mom's car and backed out the drive. I watched their taillights round the corner and disappear.

"Have you given any more thought to my proposal?" Raj asked somewhere behind me.

I turned to find him lying on my bed, flipping through the pages of my grandpa's book.

"You don't seriously think we could sneak out without getting caught, do you?"

"I don't see why not. Besides, we're old enough to take care of ourselves. In the old days we'd be considered adults right now. Even Mags. She'd probably be married already." Raj let out a soft chuckle at the prospect.

I didn't find the image amusing. Mags was far too independent to be anybody's wife. My crush aside, I couldn't help but feel that nobody else was worthy enough to stand beside her, let alone be her partner. Though I'd never say such a thing aloud. "How would we even get there? The mall is like three miles away and I don't have any money."

"Duh! We have bikes. It's not like we'd have to walk. And, happy birthday." Raj reached into his back pocket and retrieved a sealed but severely wrinkled envelope.

I knew a birthday card when I saw one. I approached and accepted the tan colored envelope, recognizing my error almost immediately.

A faint hiss echoed from inside the torn paper and a noxious gas began to fill the room.

I flailed about, trying to discard the rancid envelope. It smelled worse than the boy's locker room following gym class on Taco Tuesday. I didn't know what all was in the concoction but I could smell skunk, sweaty gym shorts, and what I guessed to be a platter of deviled eggs that had to have been left in a hot car for at least a week.

My nose burned and my eyes watered. Through the gagging I managed to pull the curtain aside enough to get the window open. Without pause I tossed the envelope outside.

Through his laughter I heard Raj shout. "Wait!"

He was off my bed and charging the window as the source of the gas descended to the ground. He peered out having suddenly lost his humor.

I have no idea how he was immune to the stench but it didn't seem to faze him.

"There was twenty dollars in there!"

It took a moment before my ability to speak returned. I suspect it had more to do with the open window than anything. As soon as my eyes cleared I found myself glaring at him. "Really, dude?"

"Yes, really. I put the money inside the card. That's what you're supposed to do."

"I'm not talking about the money. I'm talking about the stink bomb. What even was that? I've never smelled anything that bad before."

"Oh." Raj took on an innocent look paired with a sly smile. "That's a new formula I've been working on. Sweaty socks soaked in aged skunk extract. Don't worry though. I diluted it to keep it from absorbing into clothes."

"That was diluted? I'd hate to know what the full dose smells like. And no, that's not an invitation to show me." I saw the idea evaporate as quick as he'd had it.

"I'm pretty sure you wouldn't be able to smell anything else ever again. Seriously, I had one of my nose plugs slip out the other day. I can't smell a thing right now. Anyway, what are we going to do about the money?"

I shook my head. Leave it to Raj to burn out his own sniffer. "I guess we'll have to go out and get it. But I don't imagine anyone will want to accept a twenty that smells like that."

"I didn't think about that part. Still, it should air out before we get to the ice cream parlor."

"Whatever. Just leave the window open. I don't want to risk that nasty stuff lingering."

We hurried to the door and rushed downstairs. The living room TV was turned on and blaring some game show. I didn't care enough to see which one it was. As the stairs opened up to reveal the lower rooms, I was surprised to find the living room empty.

I rounded the bottom banister post with Raj right behind me. "Grandpa, are you here?"

"In here." Grandpa's voice echoed from the other side of the dining room.

I followed through into the kitchen.

Grandpa was standing near the central island with a paper plate fully loaded with a triple decker sandwich and a pile of potato chips. "You boys eaten anything yet?"

"Not yet." I was impressed. I'd only attempted the triple decker myself a few times and it never went well. There was something about three pieces of bread, double meat, double cheese, lettuce, tomato, and whatever else he'd piled inside that made it a beautiful work of art. A part of me wanted to try it but a bigger part simply wanted to escape.

"My mom ordered us pizza." Raj added. "It should be here soon."

"I see. Well, if you get hungry before then, you know where the kitchen is."

I can't say I found Grandpa's statement amusing but at that moment a few thoughts came to mind. First, we were standing in the kitchen. Of course we knew where it was. Second, this wasn't his house, yet he acted as if it were. And lastly, was he attempting a grand dad joke by inviting me to use the kitchen of my own home?

I decided the best response would be an honest one that was open enough to get us out of there. "Thanks, Grandpa, but Raj and I need to go outside for a few minutes."

"Oh, yeah. We'll only be a minute." Raj added, as if he'd forgotten why we'd come downstairs in the first place.

"Okay. But don't be sneaking off. It's getting dark. No telling what sorts of things could be out there just waiting for a couple of boys to happen by." Grandpa gave us a mischievous smile.

I couldn't help but feel maybe he'd overheard Raj's plans. "We'll be right back."

Leaving Grandpa to his sandwich, I turned and made for the front door.

My bedroom was in the upstairs corner of the house, overlooking both the driveway and garage. From the window I'd opened the envelope should have landed somewhere near the driveway.

I opened the door and stepped out. The sudden presence nearly took my breath away.

I don't know if it was what Grandpa had said or if whatever had followed me from the retirement home had found me, but the moment I crossed the threshold my fear returned.

I knew it was there, somewhere, watching from a distance, ready to strike.

"I think that's it over there." Raj pointed across the driveway, toward my dad's car. He darted around me as if nothing was wrong and slipped into the shadows.

I couldn't focus enough to look where Raj was searching. My sight was locked on whatever it was across the street. Even with the full moon I felt like I was standing in total darkness. The porch light, which was always on, was now inexplicably dark. I could have blamed it on a burnt bulb, or maybe Grandpa hit the wrong switch, but it seemed more nefarious than that. The path from the driveway to the front porch was lined with solar lights and none of those were on either.

I could hear Raj on the other side of my dad's car. He didn't seem to have a care in the world. Maybe I was simply going crazy.

"No, this is just a broken foam cup." He shook his head inspecting the refuse. "I'll never understand how people can just throw their trash on the ground. It's not that hard to put it in a trash can."

He stepped out of my view but from the sound I knew he'd approached the blue plastic dumpster just past the garage where our bikes were parked.

Finally, I gained enough of my senses to speak. "You see the card anywhere?" I wanted to help but I knew there was no hope for me if I stepped out the protection of the front porch.

"Not yet. Why am I the one looking anyway? You're the one who threw it out the window."

"I'm not the one who laced it with skunk spray."

"Fair enough." Raj began cackling a second time.

"What are you losers doing out here? Oh my god, what's that smell?" As if a glowing light burned through the center of darkness, Mags appeared on the walkway leading to the front door. The sight of her fair skin and wavy hair began to evaporate my fear.

I'd been so focused on the thing in the dark that I nearly jumped when I saw her. I turned, hearing her chuckle at my embarrassment.

Her features were barely visible in the low light but I could still make out the freckles crowning her nose and cheeks.

"Raj thought it would be funny to give me a birthday card rigged with a stink bomb. I threw it out the window."

"It has twenty dollars in it!" Raj declared from around the corner. His silhouette came back into view, seemingly hunched over and staring at the ground.

"Find it yet?"

"I wouldn't still be looking if I did."

Mags sighed. "Idiots!"

I don't know if it was my mind playing tricks on me or if it was actually happening, but as Mags approached my vision seemed to clear. I could see further, like it wasn't as dark. That wasn't as calming as I hoped it would be.

Just on the other side of the chain link fence, beyond where Raj was searching the ground, I could plainly see a dark figure standing there watching us. It had but to reach out and it'd have him. I was frozen. My mind was locked on the sight. I couldn't scream. I couldn't warn him. I couldn't do anything.

He was helpless and I was stuck there watching my best friend wander blindly into the clutches of a monster.

"Are—are you okay?" Mags asked. A look of concern was blatant across her face. I felt comfort in her presence, like a warmth engulfing me. She made the world brighter.

No sooner than her foot touched the porch all the lights came to life and the dark figure was gone.

I let out a breath, unaware I'd been holding it. I searched the surrounding area, looking for whatever it was I'd seen. It was nowhere to be found. My heart continued to pound but my panic settled.

Realizing Mags was staring at me, I found my voice. "I—um, yeah. Sorry, I don't know what happened. I guess I got carried away. I felt like I was being chased earlier today. I thought whatever it was, was back."

"You should go inside." Mags offered, studying my features. She pressed her hand to my forehead as if checking for a fever. I have to admit it felt pleasant.

"He can't go in yet. We have to find the money. And then we have things to do. If we go in we may not be able to come out again."

"What's he talking about?"

"My parents forgot my birthday. They left for a trip a little while ago. Raj thinks we should sneak out and go to that new ice cream place on the strip."

"Are you guys kidding me? That's like five miles away. Not to mention you'd be in big trouble if you got caught. And what about game? It's not like I've been preparing this for two weeks or anything."

"I didn't say we were going." I pleaded, hoping to escape her wrath. Mags was always the responsible one in our group. I was glad to have her around when Raj got one of his ideas.

"You didn't *not* say." Raj retorted, holding up the torn envelope. "And now that I found the money, there's nothing to stop us." He waved the envelope for good measure.

"Look, I'm not going to tell you guys what to do, but I came over here to game. I'm going inside. If you want to be immature children, continue with this stupid plan. If not, I'll see you at the table." Without another word, Mags stepped past me and disappeared inside.

I glanced to Raj, hoping he'd gotten the message. Judging by the fact he was still waving the envelope at me with a stupid grin on his face I suspected otherwise. "Come on, Raj. It's not like any of us want to ride that far after dark anyway." I turned to follow Mags.

"But—but—Oh, all right." Raj crossed the pavement and joined me just as I crossed the threshold.

Mags was already setting up when we got to the dining room. The chandelier was faintly illuminated, casting a dim glow over a large tiled map she'd spread across the table.

She had her GM screen set up at the windowed end and arranged to block her area from the rest of us. A stack of books sat neatly to her left and a pile of purple and gold dice rested to her right.

The map was decorated with various colored lines detailing a rather intricate floorplan to what I could only assume was a keep of some kind. Miniature monsters were gathered in the corner nearest the GM screen, awaiting use, and a row of dry erase markers rested in a tray with the letters R.O.Y.G.B.I.V. drawn beneath each slot.

She didn't look up as we took our seats but I suspected she was silently celebrating her victory.

Mags opened a plastic clipboard and retrieved two character sheets and handed one to each of us. "Since we're gaming here this week, I assume Ananya isn't joining us?" She asked Raj.

"No. But it's no big loss. She'd rather rob everyone for their clothes than help us anyway."

"She's six. What did you expect her to do?" Mags retorted with a smile.

I liked Raj's sister but I had to admit she was kind of annoying to game with. Between the constant clarification of rules, attacking anything and everyone, including our characters, and always making the story about her, we barely made any progress when she was at the table. But that was the price of gaming at Raj's house, and one of the many reasons I was glad when I hosted it.

"Okay. I haven't heard from anyone else, so game is going to be a little different with just you two. I'll play Ananya's character since she's not here. I've also made an NPC to help but I've limited it to third level so you guys won't depend on it."

"Oh, do I have time to grab the spell book my grandpa gave me? I think there might be some cool new spells I can retrofit."

"I'll need to review them before casting but I'll allow it. Just remember you only have a few spell slots available."

I nodded and got to my feet. It took only a moment for me to run to my room, grab the book off my bed, and return to the table.

"That doesn't look like any spell book I've ever seen." Mags commented, studying the size of the massive tome. "What game is it from?"

"I don't know. I can't read the cover but I know it's old. Probably a first edition."

"Whatever. Let's get started." Mags waited for me to take my seat before she began.

"To recap, last game you were navigating the Temple of Carnyth. Ananya found the lever which opened a passage into the catacombs. Raj, you disturbed the alter and awoke a dark god who'd been imprisoned there. As the dead were rising from their graves, you guys decided to flee back to the Tavern in Westbrook rather than fight. We called it a night there. Any questions?"

"Yeah. Did I get my health points back?" Raj asked, studying his character sheet.

"You got a full night's rest and regained one hit die plus your Con modifier worth of points. Any used spell points or abilities have reset."

Raj rolled a d6 and quickly added the numbers.

I did the same only more discretely.

"Both of you awake to the morning sun glaring through the thick glass of the tavern's dirty windows. The smell of cooking meat radiates from downstairs. It's a sweet scent, like maple bacon and pancakes. As the visions of the previous night fill your mind, you recall there were only two rooms available, both even numbers. I need you both to attempt an Intellect check."

"Eight." Raj announced defeated.

"Sixteen."

"Raj, the smell of food makes your stomach growl with hunger."

"I get up and grab my things before heading downstairs."

"Okay. Aaron, as you're lying in bed trying to decide whether you should get up or not, you suddenly recall the room numbers being staggered from your first visit here. Odd numbers were on the east and even on the west. From this room, you shouldn't be able to see the morning sun. Moreover, you know what bacon smells like. This doesn't smell like bacon."

"I jump to my feet and grab my pack. Cautiously, I place my hand against the door and feel for heat."

"It's hot. Raj, in your hurry to get food you unbolt the door and yank it open. I need you to attempt a Reflex save as flames explode into your room from the burning hallway."

"Ha—Evasion!" Raj demanded, rolling his d20. "*Natural twenty, I can move mountains!*" He began to sing.

"Seeing the flames, you instinctively spin and shield yourself with the door as the backdraft washes into the room. The heat wave goes right past you, leaving you untouched. You have two rounds before the flames consume all the oxygen in the room and you'll start taking negatives to rolls."

"I pull my bandana over my face to protect against the smoke and look for a way out."

"Okay. Aaron what are you doing?"

"Question, if I were to cast Wind Shield, would it push the flames away from me or cook me like a convection oven?"

Mags thought for a moment. "That's the one that's like a small tornado that surrounds you?"

"Yeah."

"High or low?" She rolled her dice behind the screen.

"Er—low?"

"You haven't seen the flames yet, but you're fairly certain if the hallway is engulfed, the suction would be more powerful than the force and it would likely pull the heat to you even if it pushed the flames away."

"Okay. What would I have to do to increase the duration of Gust of Wind?"

"What is it now?"

"One round, straight-line blast of strong winds. I want to turn it into a concentrated cone so I can get to Raj."

Mags nodded her understanding. "You think if you empower the spell, your gust might just be strong enough to extinguish the flames in the upstairs hall."

"Would that clear a path to his room?"

"It should, but it's also going to make it hotter."

"Okay. I do that." I calculated the spell points for the empowered spell and marked my sheet.

"You prepare your spell, forcing every ounce of concentration into it. Timing it just right you let it loose and open the door at the same time. The fire swirls violently right outside your room, fighting against the strong winds. The heat is nearly unbearable and you can smell your clothes starting to burn. Just when you think you can't take anymore, the wind breaks through. The flames implode on themselves with a boom. You stand there, collecting yourself as wisps of smoke gently drift off your robes.

"The hallway is severely charred and several spots are glowing embers but it looks like it's safe to step into the hall."

"Do I notice this?" Raj asked.

"Make a Perception check."

"Eighteen."

"A deafening roar echoed outside your room. Then, suddenly, a strong breeze blew past you and you heard a loud woof as the flames went out. Most of the fire, at least here, is gone for now but you can still see a few lingering flames and hear the popping of the smoldering wood."

"I carefully step around the door and go into the hallway."

"After I've made sure my eyebrows are still there, I'm going into the hallway too." I added.

"You two see each other, both a little singed but not the worse for wear. I need both of you to attempt Memory checks."

"Fourteen" I answered, adding my d20 to my memory stat.

"Eight." Raj pouted, replacing the die with another like it.

"Aaron, you just realized Ananya's character isn't with you. You remember a huge argument about which room she was claiming. She insisted since you two were boys you should room together and she should have the other to herself, but you don't remember anything beyond that point. In fact, you don't remember going up to the rooms."

"Do I remember this?" Raj asked.

"No. You rolled an eight. You don't remember where you left your daggers."

"I do too. They're on my—" Raj paused, inspecting his character sheet. "They were written right here. Did—did you erase them?"

Mags sighed. "You tried to pry a stone door open with one last game and it got broke. The other you threw at a skeleton and never retrieved it before you fled."

"This sucks." Raj demanded, resting his head on the table.

"What you kids doin'?" Grandpa asked, carrying his now empty plate toward the kitchen.

"Gaming." I answered hoping he wouldn't question it further. To my fortune he paused long enough to look over the table before continuing past.

"No out of character talking, Raj." Mags taunted.

I couldn't help but notice she seemed to take a small amount of joy in tormenting him from time to time. Of course, he usually brought it upon himself with one of his pranks, or schemes, or general tomfoolery if that was still a word people used.

"As you two are standing there, one reflecting on the missing memories of the night before, the other looking helpless with his sudden realization of disarmament, you hear a soft giggle that sounds like it's in the air around you."

"Like a maniacal giggle?" I asked, imagining some Team Rocket punk taking delight in a momentary victory.

"No. It's more like a child. Female."

"Where's it coming from?" Raj asked, picking himself up.

"You're not sure. It sounds like it's all around you, both in the hall and inside your head. No matter which way you look it sounds like it's directly behind you."

"That's creepy!" Raj demanded, looking behind him for good measure.

"I need you both to attempt Perceptions."

"Twelve."

"Twelve."

"You both feel the floor sink a little. If you had to guess, the lower level is still on fire and the braces are about to give."

"Finding the nearest window." Raj exclaimed.

"You step back into your room and notice the flames have climbed the outside wall. There's no way you're going to be able to escape out these windows without getting burned or worse."

"Then I'll pick the lock on one of the closed doors and check the other side."

"You start to mess with the lock and realize the flame has badly charred the wood. It'd be faster to simply bust the door in."

"Okay. I kick the door open."

I sat quietly, observing the story. There wasn't much my character could do in the way of physical abilities. I was better at quick thinking and flinging spells at my problems.

"The door groans under the force and starts to split where the hinges are fixed. Attempt a Fortitude save."

"Do I need to make one too?"

"Are you looking into the room?"

"Yes."

"Then yes. Both of you need to roll."

"Sixteen!" Raj announced with pride.

"Seven."

"Aaron, you're standing there watching him kick open the door. No sooner than it rips away from its hinges and falls inside, your vision locks onto what appears to be a whole family arranged at the center of the small room. You aren't entirely sure what's happened to them. Their skin has been peeled away and is decorating the wooden floors with chunks of organ and a thick layer of ichor. You're unable to do anything as you double at the waist and vomit what little food you had the night before.

"Raj, you're staring at the grizzly scene and you're not sure but it looks like these people were used in some kind of ritual sacrifice. There's a crude alter at the center of their placement and it looks like their blood was used to mark the sigils on the floor and walls."

The doorbell rang causing me to jump.

"Are you expecting others?" Grandpa yelled from the kitchen. I could hear his voice growing louder which told me he was headed back this way.

"No one else said for certain they were coming." I rushed to the door and stole a glance out the peep hole. It was dark as could be on the other side. That told me the porch light was out again.

Cautiously, I pulled the door open and looked around. I was starting to think something was terribly wrong.

"Are you Aaron?" A voice asked out of the darkness and I jumped nearly ten-foot in the air.

The man's face appeared, wreathed in shadow and I could tell he was trying not to laugh. He was holding a red box of some kind and I instantly knew his purpose.

I took a deep breath to settle my nerves before speaking. "I am." My stomach growled at the prospect of fresh pizza.

"I was asked to deliver—this!" The pizza guy lunged forward with a large knife in his hand.

I stumbled backward and tripped over my feet, falling to the floor just inside the door.

He howled with laughter, trying to stop himself. "It's—it's all right, kid." His laughter continued in spurt. "It's a fake knife." He stabbed his hand with it and the blade retracted inside the handle.

"Oh, man. Did I miss it?" Raj asked, coming up behind me. "You were supposed to wait for me to be here. It would have been more convincing."

"Sorry." The pizza guy handed the prop knife to Raj and went to work retrieving the pizza from its carrier.

"That's not funny! How would you like it if some stranger fake stabbed you?" I wasn't sure who I was talking to. I guess it was more to the general assembly. I was just glad Mags and Grandpa hadn't seen it. It was bad enough Raj knew about it. Of course, it sounded like he'd had a hand in its orchestration.

"Don't be such a wuss." Raj accepted the pizza boxes and stared down at me.

"It's okay kid. Happy birthday by the way. They paid me an extra twenty for the prank." The pizza guy turned, still chuckling to himself and disappeared back into the night.

Climbing to my feet I shut the door and glared at Raj. "No more jokes tonight. I've had enough."

"Okay. I promise no more jokes."

We returned to the dining room to find Grandpa sitting at the table with a character sheet in hand. His glasses were narrowly fixed to the tip of his nose and his eyes darted across the pencil written stats.

"Um, what's happening?"

"Your Grandpa was curious about the game. I told him he could play." The glare in Mags' eyes dared me to object.

"But—but—he doesn't have a character. How can he play?"

"He has the NPC I made. Don't worry. The story will work fine."

"Whatever." I gave in and plopped into my seat.

# Chapter 4
## Slipping Reality

Raj set the stack of pizza boxes on the center table, covering the map. He immediately opened the top box. "Mom got us pepperoni, sausage, and cheese."

He grabbed a slice of pepperoni and took his own seat, snaking a string of melted cheese into his mouth before taking the first large bite.

I grabbed a slice of pepperoni and a slice of sausage and pressed the two faces together to form a triangle shaped sandwich. It was the next best thing to rolling one of those cheap personal pizzas into a burrito and eating it that way, though I have to admit it was much better when they were round instead of square.

"Okay. Now that the interruptions are over, can we continue our game?" Mags grabbed a slice of cheese and retreated behind her screen.

Chewing a rather large mouthful of pizza sandwich, I nodded.

Judging by her expression, I assume Raj did as well.

"Good. As I was explaining; the room is filled with bodies that appear to have been sacrificed in a most gruesome manner. Aaron, you're finally able to pick yourself up but you still feel sick. Raj, you've entered the room to investigate.

"Mister Corey, you've traveled by horse for several days now, stopping at the various towns and settlements along the way. Your order has had no contact from this region in almost six months. They sent you to investigate. You left last night's camp well before sunrise and have ridden hard for a couple hours. The morning is chilly and dark, with storm clouds overhead. You sense it's going to rain soon but it hasn't started yet. Make me a Perception check."

"How do I do that?"

Raj leaned over and pointed out the skill tree listed along the lower right half of the character sheet. Talking through pizza mouth, he gestured to the pile of borrowed dice in front of my grandpa and showed him the d20. "Woll dat one an add da number to your Perception skill."

"Oh, okay." Grandpa rolled the die and announced. "Sixteen!"

"As you crest a hill you see a fair-sized town off in the distance. Your map tells you it's called Westbrook and it's the last trade post for nearly a week's travel by caravan. You also know your order has a small convent here but like the others this side of the Corinthian Mountains, no correspondence has been received in quite some time."

"I'll go into the town." Grandpa replied, taking the silence as his que.

"It takes a little bit to reach but as you near the town gate the scent of smoke reaches your nose. This wouldn't be all that uncommon if not for the strength of it. Instinctively, you glance around in search of the source. Almost immediately, you spot an orange glow in the clouds toward town center. What do you do?"

"Um, well, an orange glow usually means a fire. And the smell of smoke confirms it. Is there a fire department I can call or do I need to handle this like when I was a kid and gather the townsfolk to haul buckets of water?"

I sighed. "It's a medieval setting, Grandpa. There isn't a fire department."

"Oh, okay. So, considering sunrise happens around six and I've been riding for a few hours, I'm going to assume it's around eight. People should be up and about. I'm going to spur my horse into a quick trot but keep it from a gallop. Wouldn't want anyone to step in front of me and get trampled in all the chaos. As I pass buildings and people, I'll yell 'fire' as I make my way toward the source."

"It takes you a couple minutes to navigate the roads, dodging people as they step out to see what the commotion is about. After a few rows of buildings, you break through into the town square where you get your first glimpse as to just how severe it really is.

"Several buildings are fully ablaze. People are rushing about, trying to decide what to do. I need you to attempt an Animal Handling check to see how well you're able to keep your horse under control with all the confusion of flame and people."

Grandpa scanned the skill list. Repeating the steps from his last check, he rolled the d20 and added the numbers. "Twelve!"

"Despite your best effort your horse just isn't having it. With all the people around and the smoke and flame and heat, you're having trouble getting the horse to continue toward the commotion. It comes to a full and complete stop and you almost lose your grip on the reins. Just as you're about to leave the saddle and go flying over the horse's head, you manage to dig your heels in and hold fast. In all the excitement you hadn't noticed before, but now that you're stopped you smell a strange scent in the air. Something more than just cloth and wood. Something doesn't belong."

"What is it?"

"You aren't sure. You can smell the burning buildings clear as day but there's something else mixed in. Something sweet but nauseous at the same time. Go ahead and roll another Perception for me."

"Nine."

"There isn't much wind to carry the smoke away. Instead, it's billowing down and fanning over the area, blocking much of your sight. You think you can see people moving about in the distance but the smoke is lingering like fog, getting thicker moment by moment and you can't make out the details."

"I'm going to climb off my horse and hitch him somewhere safe before walking closer to the buildings."

"Okay. I'll get back to you in a few minutes. Raj, what are you doing?"

"Eating pizza." He joked through a mouth full.

The glare Mags gave him said more than words. With a simple glance she spurred him into action.

"I'm looking for any specific marks or sigils that might say who this sacrifice was to."

"Do you have any ranks in Knowledge Religion?"

"No."

"You can roll an Intellect check but you're going to take a minus four."

"Ha, negative two." Raj chuckled and slid his d20 back into the pile, selecting another.

"You've never seen sigils like these before. I need both you and Aaron to attempt Reflex saves."

We rolled and I instantly found myself wishing I had evasion. "Nine."

"Nineteen!"

"The floor shifts beneath your feet. You're fairly certain it dropped a few inches and you can see flames dancing between the growing gaps in the floorboards. You're certain the gaps weren't that wide a moment ago. Aaron, the sudden jolt knocked you off balance and you landed on your back. You can feel the heat radiating through the wood. Roll me a d4."

I grabbed one of my pyramid shaped dice and rolled it. "Three."

"You take three points as the burning embers from the wood press against your flesh. You'll take 1 d4 fire damage every round until you get up."

"I'm getting up."

"Roll another d4 since it will take you at least a round to stand, not to mention you have nothing to grab hold of."

I rolled, releasing a sigh as the die landed on four. I didn't bother announcing. There was no point. I just updated my hit points, wishing I'd played something with a bigger hit pool.

Mags rolled something behind her screen and continued talking. "Mister Corey, you're cautiously walking through town, searching for anyone to help put out the flames. Unfortunately, it doesn't look like most of the buildings are going to be able to be saved. To make matters worse, you aren't seeing anyone who can help. Each time you think you see someone their silhouette disappears into the ever-thickening smoke."

"Is there anything I can do to make the smoke go away? Or maybe put out the fires? Is there a water trough or reservoir? Maybe a well or something like that. You said I was a magic using class. Is there anything I can do with magic?"

"A paladin is restricted to certain types of spells. The closest your character might have is Create Water, but that's more for drinking rather than fighting a big fire. At your level, you could create a maximum of six gallons per casting. I'll allow you to roll a percentile to see if your god takes favor on you."

"How do I do that?"

"Roll both of those." Mags pointed at two d10s, one with a single digit and the other with double digits.

Grandpa lifted the pair and rolled them across the table.

"That's sixty-eight. As you're silently praying for guidance, you feel an overwhelming sense of dread form in your gut. You've felt such a thing before but never this strong. And never this all-consuming. As you recall what brought such a feeling in the past, you gasp as understanding crosses your mind.

"The negative energies which animate undead feel like a taint upon your very existence. They make you physically and spiritually ill. It's a wrongness in the world that you, being a paladin of Sulis, are obligated to right. You've never felt this much negative energy in one place before. Whatever is causing it is not only strong but numerous."

"What's causing it?"

Mags suppressed a chuckle. "I can't tell you that. You'll have to find out for yourself."

"Am I on my feet yet?" I was starting to get annoyed. I know Grandpa was just curious about our game but my entire night so far had been ruined and he was intruding where I didn't want him.

"Yes. You've gotten back up and are entering the room. Do you have Knowledge Religion?"

"I do." Grandpa interjected, seeing the name in his skill tree.

"You aren't with them currently but if you end up in a place to use it, I'll let you know."

I scanned my skills for good measure but I knew I didn't have it. I was a wizard. My knowledge skills were targeted toward arcana. Religion was for people not powerful enough to make stuff happen on their own. "No."

"Okay. Aaron, you step into the room just as the floor begins to buckle. Both of you know it isn't going to hold much longer."

"Is the fire raging outside this window?" Raj asked as if he'd just remembered why we'd come to this side in the first place.

"No. You can see the glow but the windows are still intact. It doesn't appear to have breached this outer wall just yet."

"I'm going to break the glass and climb out."

I wasn't seeing many other options. It seemed silly to flee when there was clearly something of importance right here but I didn't know what I could do. I was on limited time and the only hope of survival appeared to be out the window and away from whatever Mags wanted us to find. "I'm going to the window as well."

Habitually, I flipped through my character sheet and located my spell list. I knew there wasn't anything that would help us. And unless Raj found a safe escape we were both going to fall through the floor. Still, I wasn't one to simply give up. I was determined to find an alternative that would prolong our stay and allow us to discover whatever it was we were supposed to figure out.

My prepared spells were next to useless in our current situation. I took a deep breath and turned to the book Grandpa had given me. Flipping to a random page near the center I began scanning its contents.

Most of the words were nonsense but a few symbols held just enough meaning for me to get the basis of their intent. *Plasma bolt, energy shield, commune with dead.* I read each to myself thinking over the possibilities. What was more surprising, I had no idea how I was understanding the words. They were still just as much gibberish now as they had been before but somehow I knew what they meant.

I paused, thinking over the *commune with dead* one. If I could use that perhaps I could ask these people what had happened here. If it worked anything like the *commune with dead* in the PHB I didn't think there was time to prepare the spell.

"I see you've opened your present." Grandpa said, staring intently. He had a serious look on his face I'd never seen before.

"Yeah?"

"I urge you to be careful with that book. Many secrets lay within. I'd hate for you to stumble upon one by accident."

Mags rolled a handful of dice and a subtle smirk appeared only to be replaced by a stern expression. "Raj, you elbow the window, breaking out the glass. Before the falling pieces can hit the ground you feel the building pop and the floor starts to break apart. The temperature instantly rises as flames pour through the openings and engulf the walls around you. I need both you and Aaron to make Reflex saves, and be warned, if you fail there is only one more round before the entire place is going to implode."

I hated when she adopted that demeanor. It usually meant things were about to go bad and she would be the first to say 'I told you so'. Still, she always had the best of intentions. I couldn't fault her for it, even if I acted like I did sometimes.

I hesitated on the *commune with dead* spell again. That still didn't feel like the one I needed, though if Mags would allow it, I suspected it would grant some answers. That was provided I had time to cast it, not to mention time to ask my questions. What I really needed was a time stop or some kind of temporal shield to place the area in stasis until I could get the answers I needed.

As if my thoughts had triggered it, a gust of wind appeared out of nowhere and the pages turned of their own accord. I tried to settle them before they changed but was a moment too late. My hand flattened the page and I froze, staring at the perfect spell. It was almost like the book had magically known what I was looking for.

"There are two spells I'd like to cast. The first is an instant. The second takes a standard round. First, do I have enough time? And second, will you permit me the use of—" I scribbled the spell in question onto a scrap paper and handed it to Mags.

She scanned my writing and I could see the wheels turning. She was considering my request as I knew she would. That was the danger of it. Even if I used the version straight from the PHB it was a dangerous game that could backfire if I didn't speak the exact combination of words needed to achieve my goal. I wasn't overly thrilled with how vague my request was. I knew she'd find some way to twist it, but I also couldn't give her any fuel to out think me before I'd formally made my request.

Her eyes darted up from the paper and a wicked smile formed on her lips. "Yes, to both."

"I cast Contingency as an instant with the listed spell, and Time Stop as my standard action." I rolled my d4, calculating how long the time stop would last.

"You feel the world around you slow to a near stop. The dancing flames cease their flicker. The collapsing floor which was breaking and crumbling into the inferno beneath your feet has halted midfall. To your knowledge, you're they only being in existence able to move freely at this moment. What are you doing?"

"First, I want to steal a glance at Raj. Is there any path or way for him to safely escape without me directly affecting him?"

"You look out the window and see there's a wooden flower box just outside. One could possibly dangle from it and drop to a lower awning. But no, there's no way to get him in such a position without moving him, which would break your time stop."

"What? Come on. How am I supposed to escape if I can't do anything?" Raj pleaded, searching his character sheet for anything he could use.

Mags raised a finger, silencing him.

"I want to cast Clairvoyance to find out what happened to these people and why they were sacrificed."

"What's your spell bonus?"

"Bonus or Save DC?"

"Bonus."

"Eight." I wasn't sure where she was going with this. If there was resistance the DC would have been what she needed.

"Aaron, you cast your spell. It's a little difficult getting around your time stop but you manage. You're seeing the events of the night, shortly before you awoke. Everything's dark. You're seeing nothing but shadow in all directions. Glowing eyes and vicious teeth appear like smoke, only to be wisped away in a breeze. You feel like every pair of eyes is upon you, watching you, waiting for you to let your guard down. They could jump at any moment and tear you to pieces."

Cold sweat dripped down my spine as the story engulfed me. I couldn't swear to it but the room felt darker, smaller, like it was closing in around me. I could see shadows moving outside the windows, passing straight through the blinds like ghosts made of black smoke.

"At the center of your vision you see the people who were slaughtered in this room. They're all around you, still alive, but bound and gagged, unable to cry out, unable to flee their captor. You feel the fear coursing through their veins. You hear the racing of their hearts. It's as if you're imprisoned with them.

"A figure appears in front of you. It starts as a vague humanoid shape of smoke but solidifies before you. The fear you felt before was nothing compared to what you feel in the presence of this entity.

"You instinctively struggle to back away but are frozen in place. The figure slowly turns, the cold white of his face setting your soul on fire. A wicked smile forms on his thin lips. It's almost as if he's looking directly at you. A shadowy hand reaches out.

"I need you to make an Endurance check as a throbbing, burning pain erupts in your chest.

My heart was racing a mile a minute. I could feel it thumping deep within my chest, threatening to break free and run for the hills.

Coming to my senses, I struggled to grab my d20. Palming it, I gave it a little jiggle and tipped my hand, letting it spill out and across the table. It caught on one of its numerous corners and began to spin like a coin on edge. I watched it for a long moment waiting for it to fall. Finally it began to slow, teetering between two numbers that I could see plain as day. One would mean complete success. The other, certain failure. I watched, helpless against the result.

The die stopped, balanced perfectly on the edge, refusing to give me an answer. The nineteen wasn't a perfect roll but it was certain to save me from whatever was happening. The one on the other hand was a critical failure and one I was certain would have ill consequences.

Slowly, it started to lean. I felt the hours of my life ticking by. It toppled with the near audible sound of my shattered hopes. One.

Mags looked up from the critical failure before me. Her eyes held sympathy. "We have two ways to handle this. You can roll the failure and see if you can get above a twelve. Or I can roll and you can tell me high or low."

I appreciated the option. A critical failure was never fun for anyone. It usually meant the worse possible outcome of any situation. The fact she'd given the option meant she was willing to let me claim my own fate. If I let her roll, even though it was basically a fifty-fifty chance, she had the ability to sluff the result and either save or condemn me. I would never know for certain which. Even though my odds were lower, I had to see it for myself.

I grabbed another d20 and rolled again. It tumbled across the table coming to a stop near the center. I could have cried as the number staring back at me was another *one*. A double critical failure. I lowered my head, fearful of what was to result. A double critical failure was likely to mean a permanent handicap to my character or even death.

Raj jumped to his feet, staring in disbelief. "Oh, that sucks!"

"Roll again." Mags prompted.

I wasn't sure I wanted to. A single critical failure was bad. Two was worse. If I ended up with three, there was no way I'd survive.

Hesitantly, I grabbed another d20 and carefully tossed it, hoping for a better fate than the previous two. It spun and stopped on a four. Not quite as bad but it confirmed the second failure meaning I was still going to face both of them when, in truth, I wasn't sure I could survive even one.

Mags rolled a handful of dice and looked at me fearfully. "Aaron, the shadowy figure stares intently through the vision. You aren't sure how it can see you but you know it can. Its clawed fingers reach out and burrow into your chest. You feel an intense burning as it passes through flesh and bone. Your heart seizes as the cold grip locks around it and begins to squeeze. You take four permanent Vitality damage and another eight psychic damage. You collapse to the frozen ground, losing your concentration on the clairvoyance spell. I need you to make a Reflex at a minus four."

I rolled, defeated. There was no way I was going to survive any new damage. I had two hit points left from my original total. The vitality damage was going to lower my total hit points by at least another sixteen points. The only reason it hadn't killed me was because I'd intentionally padded it early on. I only hoped Mags would let me keep my hit points until this was said and done. If not, I was already dead.

"Six." I shook my head in disbelief and tossed my character sheet toward the center of the table. It was over. There was no way to survive whatever she had in store for me.

"In your convulsions you trip over one of the broken planks and fall backward through a gap in the floor. The frozen flames wrap around you, encasing you in an orange hue. The heat is minimal as your body burns away to ash in an instant."

I let out a sigh and sat up in my chair. There was nothing I could do.

"This game is intense." Grandpa announced, watching every action from his small corner of the table.

"You don't know the half of it." Raj added.

"Aaron—" Mags started. "—as the last pieces of your body disintegrate into nothing, you feel a shock, and suddenly you find yourself being pulled up and through the flame, back to where you were moments before you cast your clairvoyance spell. Memory of your death surges through your brain and you realize your contingency spell took effect, undoing what had been done."

"What? How? I forgot about that!" I grabbed my sheet from the center of the table, hoping to somehow salvage my dignity. I suspected it was a little too late for that.

"Had you not specified the spell to take effect when your time stop broke, it wouldn't have happened that way. You're welcome." Mags offered, making sure I was acutely aware she'd been the one to save me.

"Thank you." I quickly scanned through the book, finding the spell I should have cast from the start. "Is the time stop still in effect?"

"For the moment yes. But you only have two rounds before it ends and the building collapses on itself."

"Will you allow me to use this spell?" I quickly translated from the book onto the paper and passed it to her.

"Aaron, I wouldn't." Grandpa looked concerned.

"How many spell points do you have left?"

"Were the spells prior to my death used? And why not?" I asked each in turn. It seemed strange Grandpa was suddenly against me using the book. I could see him trying to find an answer but he was taking longer than I wanted to wait.

After a moment's silence Mags spoke. "Your spell points were used but the constitution and psychic damage have been reversed as if you'd never seen the figure."

"Okay." I quickly recalculated everything. "I have thirteen spell points left."

"This spell would cost you twelve to cast. So long as you understand that, I'll allow it."

"I do." I went to work sounding out the syllables from the book. Since I was using a foreign spell I figured I might as well include the verbal components. Truth be told, I liked the concept. If only more of the modern books contained the same. It would have made playing a caster more authentic. "Evello fila ut encompass magicae circa mundi. Movere sto ubi affectu et desiderio meo."

I felt a strange sensation rise up inside me. The lights flickered and went out and I could hear a hum in the air. Violent winds swirled around me and my vision went black.

Then, as quick as it had begun, I was standing alone in the last place I expected to be.

# Chapter 5
## A Secret World

Moonlight beamed through the heavy overcast. The rolling clouds diffused, turning what would have been a blanket of light into a soft glow that barely cut through the darkness.

I heard the crunch of leaves under my weight and could feel stalks of grass rubbing my legs in the breeze. Despite the warm weather earlier in the day, a light frost had settled on the ground. I was beginning to feel the cold on my bare arms.

I hadn't expected to end up alone and outside. I wasn't even sure how it'd happened.

Raj wanted me to sneak out. If this was some kind of elaborate prank he'd devised, I have no Idea how he managed to pull it off. It seemed beyond even his ability. He'd gone to some pretty great lengths in the past but this was far beyond anything I could even imagine.

Still, I couldn't figure out how he knew I hated this place— this evil patch of trees that had caused me so much fear. I'd never mentioned it to him before. I'd never mentioned it to anyone. Even if I could figure out how he gotten me here I didn't know how he knew about it.

Raj had a moto; *The trick to a good prank: Never let them expect it.* For the most part I'd done good to always expect it from him. But not this time, especially after what he'd had the pizza guy do.

A strong breeze wrapped around me, sending shivers down my spine. Leaves and branches rattled. I watched steam expel with my breath and disappear into the dense dark forest.

The cold, along with my growing fear, made me shiver. I rubbed my arms, trying to generate some warmth. If I'd known he was going to pull this I would have at least worn a jacket.

Crunching leaves echoed in the darkness around me. It sounded like footsteps but I couldn't be sure. They were at an even volume, just beyond sight. I had no idea if they were coming or going, as if their sole purpose was to creep me out.

"Hello? Raj? I know you're in there. This isn't funny anymore!" I wanted to be mad but I couldn't find my anger. It was blocked by my sheer terror of whatever was in the woods waiting for me.

I stared down the worn path that I'd never been able to make myself travel. I knew Grandpa's retirement home was just a short distance on the other side. If I could just make it there I'd at least have shelter and a phone. Maybe I could have someone come get me. But who could I call? My parents were gone. Grandpa wasn't at the retirement home. And both Raj and Mags were at my house.

Considering Raj had gone through the effort of stranding me out here, however he'd managed it, I wasn't about to call him. What's worse, I couldn't envision any way for him to pull it off without my grandpa and Mags being involved.

It wasn't like he could just knock me out and carry me to the place I hate most without any kind of help, especially since we were all together what seemed like seconds ago.

The footsteps I'd been listening to abruptly ended. I didn't know if whatever had been making them stopped or if it simply vanished but I wasn't too keen on finding out. In the absence of the crunching leaves and snapping twigs I suddenly realized there were no other sounds. The wind had stop rustling leaves. There were no crickets chirping or birds cawing.

It was silence in its truest form, save for the pounding in my chest that was beginning to feel like war drums threatening to tear me apart.

Despite the filtered moonlight it may as well have been pitched black beyond my immediate surroundings. I came to the realization that every creature that wanted to get me was just beyond sight.

I had nowhere to go, nowhere to run, nowhere except deeper into the forest—deeper into the one place I was certain death would claim me.

"Aaron." A melodical voice called from the darkness. It was soft and calm, like that of a young girl calling to a sibling. "Come play with us."

I had no desire to obey. If anything it made me want to run a million miles in the other direction.

"Raj, I know that's you. Quit messing around!"

"Aaron, won't you play?"

"I have a knife!" I threatened, raising my mechanical pencil menacingly.

The edge of darkness was getting closer, closing in around me. I'd had a good twenty feet of grass, weeds, and dirt between me and the towering trees, but that distance seemed to be shrinking rapidly. I estimated it was only about twelve feet away now. Eight—five—I couldn't even see the trees anymore. If the darkness got any closer I knew I'd have no choice but to run.

Game terms popped into my head.

A standard round was roughly six seconds. A regular human character could walk thirty feet in a single round, or run at maximum of one-hundred and twenty feet in that time. The statistics told me I didn't have time to analyze how fast the darkness was closing in. I didn't have time to do anything except run. If I didn't act now it would be on me before I could even hope to escape.

What was worse, I only had one direction to go and it was the last one I wanted to consider.

Before the thought had finished forming, my legs kicked into gear. The shadows were there waiting.

I could feel a cold radiance upon me. Icy fingers caressed my skin. I have no idea why they didn't lock onto me. It was like being touched by hundreds of cold, clammy hands that wanted nothing more than to feel my skin. I dodged and twisted and fought my way through, working deeper into the forest.

My *knife* was next to useless, catching nothing but air as I swung and jabbed in near panic. My feet acted of their own volition. The harder I ran the more the fingers reached for me. They pawed at my face and tugged my clothes but finally I broke through.

The moonlight must have found a break in the clouds because I could see again. Trees stood close all around. Many of their leafless branches were stretched toward me, though I know it wasn't the branches which had grabbed me.

I was standing within a ring of towering trees which seemed to be holding the darkness at bay. I couldn't see the trail anymore but I knew I was near the other side.

What had always appeared to be an impenetrable barrier from the outside was more spacious than I would have ever thought possible. My vision had shifted from normal color to more of a grayscale. Beyond the ring I could see vertical black lines in varying thicknesses that arced from the ground up into the sky. Between those lines was slightly lighter patches of gray, highlighted from the sparse light filtering through the canopy.

As frightening as it was I suddenly felt a minor comfort knowing whatever had been trying to get me couldn't follow. Unfortunately, it didn't alleviate the knowledge that something even worse, something that even the unseen monsters were afraid of, was hidden somewhere nearby.

I needed to get out of here but I didn't know what would happen if I stepped out of the ring. I didn't even know which direction to go. Beyond the silhouettes at the edge of sight was total darkness.

Knowing I couldn't stay where I was, I swallowed my fear and cautiously tested a step beyond the protective barrier. To my surprise nothing grabbed me.

A step at a time I made my way between the bark covered pillars. The semi-frozen leaves crunched underfoot. Each snap of a branch announced my location and I feared the shadows were going to grab me but none closed in like they had before.

Each branch that clung to me reminded me of the thin fingers, though these weren't icy cold. I was just glad none had held on when I fought to get free.

In the dim light I could just make out the trees as I passed. Suddenly, the ground became softer and the crunch of leaves seemed to lessen. I was glad for the change. I suspected I'd found the trail but I couldn't be certain. The trees were still as thick as ever.

An orange glow appeared ahead of me, just above face level. I could barely make it out between the trees. I started toward it like a moth drawn to flame.

As I neared details started to appear. I was able to dodge a few spider webs and branches that would have clung to my face. I skirted a large sinkhole that went down for who knew how far.

I realized I wasn't on the trail but rather something else. The path was covered in a thick moss. I fear it was one of those things that didn't exist until I'd found it.

Avoiding the numerous rocks, leaves, and sticks that had spilled onto the natural carpet, I pressed toward the light. Tree limbs seemed to grow away from me, making my trek all the more easier.

As I got closer the orange glow separated into two lights, then three. Before long I realized I was looking at an entire row of lights about chest level. The forest opened and the trees thinned into a large clearing.

I was standing at the edge of some strange cottage surrounded by a winding stone wall. The top of each post held an oddly shaped lantern that radiated the flickering lights. I then saw the strangest thing yet. The post closest to me was empty, as if awaiting its lantern.

My desire to approach was both overwhelming and frightening. I reasoned whoever lived there might have a phone. I wanted to seek shelter from the darkness. I wanted so many things the disembodied whispers promised me I'd find if I came just a little closer.

At the same time I could feel the promises were wishful thinking. Lies to lead me into a trap. I knew I wouldn't find any of my desires here. I needed to turn around and run the other direction. But where could I go? Even if I managed to get to the forest's edge I couldn't go out there. But I couldn't stay here either.

I took another step closer to the strange cottage when I suddenly realized why the place made me feel uneasy.

The fence I'd thought was made of stone had strange protrusions here and there. It looked more akin to piled bones than stone or wood. Even the lanterns were sun-bleached white with glowing light that looked like eye sockets.

As I squinted I could just make out defined cheek structures and loose teeth clinging into sockets. I knew then the fence was made entirely of human bones.

As if the revelation gave away my presence, the entire cottage jumped in the air and thin stilts that reminded me of chicken legs sprouted beneath it. It danced around and squatted back onto its foundation as if it was now staring at me.

I didn't wait to see what it was going to do next. I ran.

My feet carried me over downed logs and around blackened silhouettes and through narrow gaps of vines and thorns that tore at my clothes.

I had to get away. If I stopped I knew the thing in that house, whatever it was, was going to get me. That filled me with more dread than anything the shadow creatures had in store for me.

"A-A-Ron!" I heard through the trees.

"Raj?" I questioned aloud. Had he finally realized this prank had gone too far? Had he finally decided to tell me it was all a joke? I didn't even care if he laughed this time. I just wanted to get out of here and find the comfort of my friends, even if they were the ones that put me here to begin with.

"Aaron!" Mags shouted somewhere to my left.

I turned toward her voice. Almost instantly I broke through a row of trees and crashed into them. We tumbled to the ground in a heap.

"Ugg, A-A-Ron, get off me!" Raj groaned.

Before I could realize I was the one atop, my relief took over and I threw my arms around them. I was never so glad to see anyone in my life.

My eyes settled on Mags. She looked annoyed but didn't say anything. I suspected she had some idea as to what I'd been through. She patted my back sympathetically.

Sudden realization of what I was doing came over me and I released my hold and rolled off of them. When I got to my feet I saw my grandpa standing there, just beyond the dogpile.

"Aaron, that was a foolish thing you did. You need to be more careful. I didn't give you this book to misuse the things within!" Grandpa scolded, extending the thick tome toward me.

I was taken back. I'd never heard him use such a tone before. He was always so casual. I guess I suspected he didn't know how to be stern. What surprised me most though was why he was getting onto me. It wasn't as if I did this. It had been done to me.

I looked from Grandpa to Mags to Raj, and back again. Raj had just finished picking himself up. He had a big smile on his face. "Did you know?" he asked, fueling my confusion.

"Did I know what?"

"Duh—That magic is real!"

"I—Um—What?"

"Of course he didn't. Look at him. He's just as surprised by all of this as we are." Mags answered.

I could see compassion in her eyes. In this moment she understood me better than anyone ever had.

"Children, we don't have time for this right now. It isn't safe out here." Grandpa glanced around as if searching for something unseen. "Follow me."

Without another word he marched straight through the tree line.

I didn't want to go back into the forest but with Grandpa, Mags, and Raj I knew it would be okay this time. If nothing else, at least I had some company if things got bad.

Mags walked in after Grandpa and I followed her, letting Raj take the rear. I had so many questions and no idea how to ask them.

"How'd you do it?" Raj asked.

"How'd I do what?"

"You know. Get here."

"If you're messing with me, it isn't funny. You know I don't know how I got here. I thought you did it."

"How would I do it?"

"Duh—One of your stupid pranks! For all I know this is still some elaborate joke you're pulling. How else would you guys know where to find me? Though I still don't know how you pulled it off. I suspect some kind of knockout gas."

"Dude, I didn't have anything to do with this. We were gaming. You read that spell and the lights started flashing. Then wind started blowing. The next thing I knew you were gone. Honestly, I freaked out a little. Mags freaked out too."

"I didn't freak out. I was concerned. There's a difference."

"Sure!" Raj taunted.

"So how did you guys get here?"

"Your Grandpa brought us." Mags answered, pushing a tree branch aside for us to pass unhindered.

"How? He doesn't even have a car as far as I know."

"Dude, haven't you been listening. Magic is real! He used the same spell you did. Though I don't know how he targeted you or why it brought us here. Maybe something in the words?"

"Wait, you're telling me my grandpa has magic?"

"Yeah. He said it runs in your family and that you're supposed to be the next wizard but tonight is some kind of important night when your power is supposed to come in. That's why he arranged for your parents to leave and why he came to watch you. He said it was dangerous for you to be on your own."

"What? You mean this was all a part of—"

"I think questions are best reserved for when we're safe." Grandpa interjected as he stepped through a gap in the trees and into the opening on the other side.

A bricked wall with black iron ran the length of the road not far from where we came out. I recognized it instantly. The retirement home stood out like a vast complex of lights and buildings. Straight ahead was an electronic gate. A keypad and card scanner were embedded in the bricks beside it. There were no cameras or guard shacks watching over it as far as I could tell.

I'd passed this section of wall numerous times and I'd never once seen a gate here.

As grandpa approached the gate a small card materialized in his hand. He swiped the card and immediately began punching an absurdly long sequence of numbers into the keypad. The indicator light flashed red twice and then let out a long green pulse with a beep as the gate began to swing open on its own.

He gestured for us to enter.

The world shimmered as I stepped through the barrier. It was a much different place than I could have ever imagined.

Instead of the numerous game courts, grass covered hills, and concrete walkways I'd seen from the front entrance, the fields were filled with sights I never thought possible. We may as well have entered any number of towns straight out of our game.

The sky was a light shade of purple and riddled with twinkling stars that seemed much closer than any I'd seen before. The roads were paved with cobblestone and the smaller trails were densely packed dirt. Brooms, moving seemingly of their own accord, were hard at work sweeping the dust off the stone streets and walkways. Unlike the concrete or bricked buildings I'd grown accustomed to seeing, all of these were made of old style wood, stone, or some combination thereof.

Hooded lanterns were fixed to posts that lined the streets and others hung from chains just outside wooden doors. They had everything from taverns, general stores, blacksmiths, stables, and even a grand civic center.

Wooden signs dangled over entranceways or were fixed to posts in places. Horse drawn buggies rattled by, their occupants unseen save for the coachman atop, wearing grander renditions of the Shady Acres' staff robes. Some carriages moved absent horse or coachman, yet somehow piloted just the same.

The thing that stood out above the rest, to me anyway, was the hundreds of castle-like towers that shot into the sky. There were too many to count. Most of the towers were made of black stone, white marble, or gray granite. There were also many made of simple red brick, though there were several which were just about every color I've ever heard of, including a few colors which I hadn't.

"Um, Grandpa, where are we?"

"Welcome to Shady Acres. Home for retired witches and wizards." He extended his hands in warm greeting and a wide smile formed on his face. "Now, we need to get some place safe before I answer the numerous questions I'm sure you have."

Grandpa signaled for one of the horseless coaches like he was hailing a taxi. One came to a stop in front of us.

"Corey Tower, please."

The door opened and a set of steps unfolded.

Grandpa gestured for us to climb inside.

Mags was the first to enter. I was right behind her.

The inside was just about the nicest thing I'd ever seen. A single wide seat rested at each end of the carriage, and another ran the wall farthest from the door. The plump cushions felt more like sitting on a couch. The corners held small tables that were covered in platters of assorted fruits, meats, cheeses, and breads, and each held an ice filled bucket loaded with glass bottles of sparkling grape juice and almost every type of soda I'd ever heard of. There were luggage compartments built into the walls above our heads and flat screens mounted flush with the maroon colored walls and literally everything was trimmed in gold.

I'd only been in a limousine once when I was three. Up until now I'd never thought anything would have surpassed the level of extravagance I'd seen that day. This put that experience to shame.

"Hey, cool! I didn't know this game was out yet."

I glanced over to see Raj had a controller in his hands and was playing some first-person shooter I'd never heard of before. How he'd found a console I have no idea. I was too enthralled with what was going on around me to even worry about the tv screens.

No sooner than Grandpa climbed in behind us, the door closed and I felt the carriage start to move. It was a much subtler transition than I would have imagined, almost like riding in a car on a slow takeoff.

Grandpa took the long seat running the side wall. He knocked on wood beneath the bench and a door opened. He placed the tome he'd given me inside it and pushed the door shut. The seam disappeared as if the door was no longer there.

"What's going on, Grandpa? What's with this place?"

"Not yet. Anyone could be listening. I'll answer your questions when we reach my tower." He offered a reassuring smile but I remained unconvinced. There was too much happening and I felt completely out of the loop. A part of me wondered if I were dreaming, though even the most convincing dream I'd ever had never felt this real.

Mags pulled the curtain on the window aside and peered out. What I saw just beyond took my breath away.

I felt like I was back in the forest, only instead of towering trees, we were now in a forest of stone towers. There were thousands of them in the distance but what was more concerning, I was looking down on the roofs to many of the smaller buildings. Some were slate shingled, others in some various wood. My limited view didn't relay much more than that but one thing was certain. We were flying.

As we gained elevation I could see many of the towers had large platforms protruding from them in places. I couldn't help but think they looked like runways at an airport. I'd never flown in anything before but this certainly wasn't how I'd imagined it.

Just as I was beginning to get used to the idea of flying through some hidden medieval city, the carriage rocked like we'd hit a bump and I realized we'd landed on a platform on one of the white towers.

The Wizard's Grandson

Levi Samuel

# Chapter 6
## Corey Tower

The guideless coach coasted to a stop. I'd been in car rides with rougher transitions.

"Welcome to my home." Grandpa said, gesturing to the door.

As if his words were a password the door magically opened and the metal steps unfolded leading us out of the carriage.

Raj wasted no time. He was out the door, head turning this way and that, utterly fascinated by everything around him. Even from where I continued to sit, I could see him studying his surroundings like a child in a candy shop.

Mags, on the other hand, was more reserved. She cautiously climbed out, her every movement calculated and precise. She looked as if she were anticipating something. Like she could sense something the rest of us could not. I'd never seen her so unnerved, though she was handling it far better than I.

I didn't know what to think—or feel—or do. I was just there—floating around like a discombobulated head witnessing all the things happening around me.

I wasn't sure I could believe any of it. My inner voice kept telling me I was dreaming—that at any moment I would wake up, late for the last day of school, and all of this would have just been a horribly vivid dream where my mind was running away with itself in anticipation of my nearing birthday.

Another part knew it wasn't a dream. I'd had extremely vivid dreams before and they never felt like dreams when I was in them. I believed everything that was happening, even the insane and impossible stuff, right up to the point when I woke up and realized it was a dream. I'd never questioned it.

That was my biggest piece of evidence so far. If I were dreaming I wouldn't be questioning if this was a dream.

I pulled my conscious mind back into my body and slowly climbed out of the carriage. The smooth white stones that made the landing were larger than expected. Everything was larger than I'd expected. The outcropping that made the platform seemed more like an airport runway from where I stood. The volume of the tower itself was massive. I'd never felt so close to the stars before, as if I had but to reach up and pluck them from the sky.

The sheer white wall continued up on my right. There were no doors or windows or openings in the section I could see. Everything beyond disappeared into a dense cloud that seemed fixed in place despite the gusty breeze that carried others away.

I found the sight odd. Not only were some clouds ignoring the wind, but others seemed to linger beneath us. And some that should have hovered overhead were strangely absent. I could see the heavens with little to no effort, but the clouds and patches of fog prevented me from seeing anything but the magical town hidden within the wall of Grandpa's retirement home. From this height I should have been able to see for miles.

I heard the horseless carriage take off, pulling me back to my senses. Realizing I'd been lost in the vastness of it all, I made my way to where Mags was standing. She looked confused and a little startled. It was as if everything she'd ever believed was being called into question. I'd never seen her like this. She was so often the voice of reason—the one who always held it together when things were getting out of hand. Now, she looked as if she were having trouble rationalizing any of it.

Naturally, I asked probably the stupidest question in the history of stupid questions. "Are you okay?"

She was slow to settle her gaze on me. "Yeah. Just trying to make sense of it all. How can all of this exist and none of us knew about it? It's like our whole lives have been one big lie. We were always told magic and monsters aren't real but it turns out they are. We're the characters in our games, helpless against the vast unknown of the world around them."

I had a rare moment of wisdom. "You're forgetting one thing though."

"What's that?"

"Our characters can't have a story if we don't interact with the plot." I didn't know where it came from. It just sort of spilled out, but it made more sense than anything else that had happened so far.

She smiled and I felt in that moment that everything was going to be okay.

"A-A-Ron, Mags, you guys have got to come see this!" Raj was standing between two protruding stones at the edge of the landing. It reminded me of nothing so much as the turrets at the top of a castle's wall, not only protecting archers but providing a perfect place to land a grappling hook.

"What's up?" I approached, stealing a glance over the edge.

"We are!" Raj pointed at the world far below us. What had been full-sized or, in some cases, large buildings, were now little blips of shape and twinkling lights far in the distance.

I'd never had a fear of heights but the view unlocked it. I stumbled backward and bumped into my grandpa. He caught me before I fell and propped me back onto my feet. I noticed he was carrying the book he'd given me.

"We need to go inside. It's still not safe out here." Grandpa stepped around me and started for the tower wall.

Mags and I walked together in silence, unsure where he was guiding us. A moment later Raj came jogging up behind.

I hadn't fully understood how big the landing was until we crossed it. The stone tower only got larger as we neared the wall. What had appeared sheer at a distance was now curved and rugged where the individual mountainous stones came together. Climbing any section of it seemed an impossible tasks without drilling holes and setting pitons. The wall curved around for quite some distance but I still couldn't see any doors or openings.

Raj squeezed his way between Mags and myself and threw his arms over our shoulders. "Guys, this is awesome! Way better than a trip to the new ice cream parlor. I mean, who would have ever thought magic was real? It's just so—so rad!"

"It doesn't bother you at all?" Mags asked, rolling her shoulder to dislodge his arm.

"No. Why would it? This is the best thing that's ever happened to us. Why do you think we game? It's an escape from normal life—and now we get to live the experience. What's not awesome about that?"

"Oh, I don't know. What about the fact that Aaron almost died tonight? He disappeared in front of us. I didn't know what happen to him. And after what his grandpa told us—" Mags fell silent but I could tell she had more to say.

"Okay, Magdalene. I get you're scared but this is like a once in a lifetime sort of thing. You should try to enjoy it."

Mags stopped dead in her tracks. I could see the fury in her eyes. I was just happy it wasn't directed at me. "Don't ever call me *that* again. You know I hate that name!"

"I could say your first name." Raj taunted.

"You do and I'll punch you."

"Whatever, *Boadicea.*"

I'm not certain I'd ever seen Mags move so fast. I heard the pop before I saw her move and suddenly Raj was laying on the ground holding his chest.

"You hit me!" Raj cried.

"I told you I would!" Mags continued on, leaving me with Raj. Before I could reach down to help him up, she'd caught up with grandpa who was just reaching the stone wall.

"She hit me." Raj repeated, rubbing his chest.

"What'd you expect?"

"I don't know." Raj took my hand and pulled himself up. "I guess I thought she was joking."

"Mags doesn't usually joke. You know that." I shrugged and turned to follow. It took only a moment to reach them at the wall.

"What are we waiting for?" I asked only to be shushed.

Grandpa was staring intently at what I thought had been a flat surface. Now that I was here I realized otherwise.

Moisture hung in the air, coating everything. What had been white stone from a distance was more accurately white moss clinging to equally white granite blocks. The moss trailed the tracks between bricks, making the glossy blocks appear rugged and roughly cut. Now that I was here I could see thousands of strange carvings cut into the hard surface.

They seemed to cover every inch of the grand structure, leaving nothing untouched. How such a thing was even possible, I couldn't say. It would have taken a lifetime to carve even one of these blocks, let alone the hundreds of thousands it would have taken to build just one of the numerous towers surrounding us.

I focused on the symbols that had my grandpa's attention. Like the spell book he'd given me, the symbols began to jump out. I was starting to understand bits and pieces, though I had no idea how.

Grandpa broke his intense study and glanced at me. "A wizard's tower is unique to him."

"Or her." Mags interjected with a glance from Grandpa.

"Or her." He corrected. "To enter a tower without permission is to face all of its defenses. When I'm away I ward against everyone, including myself. There are entities in this world which can adopt not only appearance and voice, but thoughts and feelings. Though it's impossible for such an entity to completely become another in every possible way.

"Therefore, the only defense against such an imposter is by dropping all personal defenses and allowing oneself to be tried and tested on the most personal level. Any resistance will be perceived as hostile intent and met with equal force."

Yellow lights began to glow from Grandpa's fingers. They traced the gaps around several of the blocks, weaving in and out of the multitude of symbols scattered across the surface. Within a few seconds they'd traced a full circle several feet tall and equally wide. Every sigil within began to glow a vibrant yellow and the wall melded into itself revealing an open entryway.

Grandpa stepped aside and gestured for us to enter.

Mags entered first but I was right behind her. There was a charge in the air the moment I crossed the threshold. I can't be certain if it was the warm air that greeted my cold flesh or something more sinister, but I felt conflicted. A part of me wanted to get out of this place as fast as possible while the other assured me I would never find any place safer.

Judging from the expression on both Raj and Mags' faces, they were feeling the same.

"This way." Grandpa swept around us and started down a narrow hall.

A rumble behind us drew my attention and I turned to watch the stones shift and move. In an instant the entrance where we'd come through had sealed itself as if it were never there.

We hurried after grandpa and in no time we were traveling long corridors, rounding bends, and exploring what I knew had to be little more than a small percentage of the total estate. We walked for what seemed like hours.

The walls and floors, which had begun as nothing more than coarse stone, slowly began to transition. Some halls were floored in marble or granite. Some were wood or stone. Some were carpeted or thrown with rugs to break the monotony of footsteps. Some walls held hanging tapestries while others were bare. There were fixed torches, oil lamps, flaming basins, or wall mounted electric lights located in different sections. Occasional shelves appeared here and there, loaded with odd decorations. Stone ceilings would sometimes give way to wooden beams and rafters, or in places become vaulted in elegant and exotic materials to which I couldn't identify. I even saw rooms build from modern technology and materials. The design was as chaotic as it was grand and I felt it had a single purpose—to confuse anyone who was here uninvited.

I wasn't sure which areas I liked more. The grand castle look was something I'd always been attracted to but it felt so foreign, especially with how the rest of the night had gone. The modern style was more comfortable, a little too comfortable. It made it easy to accept that none of this was real and we were simply having a shared hallucination.

Of course the small bits of magic happening all around us made sure we couldn't forget it completely, but it was an unexpected comfort nonetheless.

After what felt like an entire night of walking, Grandpa finally came to a stop at a wide archway. The room beyond was larger than my entire house. The central wall opposite where we stood was a grand and glowing fireplace with a set of three horns hanging above it. The side walls I could see were covered with book loaded shelves. A central area where the floor was lower held a long table. The wooden surface was completely bare save for a white laced cloth and large golden bowl at its center. Eight chairs were pressed comfortably beneath each of the long sides and two were tucked under the shorter edges.

Around the room numerous reading chairs, each wrapped in a different colored leather, were angled to watch the fireplace. A wooden end table sat next to each with a lamp of some kind and a few stacked books piled here and there. It was as if someone had followed the same routine in each chair, unsure which one was their favorite.

In a few places the sparse wall space between shelves was decorated with odd assortments of trophies. The top layer to one particular stand held what I guessed to be a dragon's head, though the fact that it could even fit in such a space made it much smaller than I would have imagined.

Multiple swords and shields and other weaponry were displayed here and there on racks which remained easily accessible but out of the way.

I couldn't help but notice the open balcony that wrapped the entire perimeter overhead. Wooden rails and support beams separated whatever was up there and a single staircase broke the perimeter. It made it feel larger than it already was. I was now certain my entire school could fit inside this one room.

A loud clap drew my attention to the center table. Grandpa had somehow spanned the distance and was now standing at the far end. The book he'd given me rested on the table in front of him. Dust drifted through the air, displaced from where the book had landed.

"Won't you children join me for a little education. I assure you we're safe here. At least for now."

The was something about the way he said it that left me unnerved. If this place was safe to begin with, how could it not be so later? The look on his face, a face that had never seemed as old as it did in this moment, told me whatever he had to say was worth listening to.

I had no idea what else to do. I approached and took the end seat of the long side, nearest grandpa.

Mags took the seat to my left and Raj rounded the table to sit directly across from me.

Waiting for us to get comfortable, Grandpa took the seat before him. He placed his elbows on the table and interlocked his fingers. Looking over his crescent shaped glasses, a warm gaze fell on me. "Aaron, my boy, I fear this to be a night you won't soon forget."

It seemed an odd statement to make. With everything that had happened such an announcement was quite obvious. Still, I could tell he wanted to say more but was searching for the right words. Whether it was an attempt to hold back certain information or to keep from overloading me with a bombardment, I couldn't say. I just knew he was thinking carefully about his next words.

Casually, Grandpa reached out and opened the book he'd given me. I didn't know to which page he'd turned but he seemed content in its selection and slid the entire tome toward me. "Can you read this?"

I pulled the book closer and stared intently at the scribbles scattering the page. As before it was gibberish, only this time it didn't seem to want to make sense. "I—I don't know."

"How did you read the other page?"

"I don't know. I didn't know what any of it meant. It just sort of popped into my head."

Grandpa nodded as if I'd answered an unspoken question though his gaze told me he was still awaiting an answer.

After a long moment of silence, feeling as if he were testing me, I looked away from the book. "I can't read it. What's it say?"

"I don't know. It's not my book." Grandpa answered as if that was supposed to reassure me.

"But you gave it to me. How can you not read it?" I glanced to Mags and Raj hoping for some backup but they seemed just as confused as I.

"I can understand pieces, much the same way you were able to understand the meanings earlier this evening. A wizard's spell book is as unique as the wizard himself. No wizard is capable of reading and understanding the book of another. This book is yours. Everything within it is intended for you and you alone. But you must claim it. That's why you cannot read this page. You have not claimed it yet." Grandpa tapped the open page for emphasis.

"There has to be some kind of mistake. I'm not a wizard. I only play one in our game. I don't even know how to read spells or use magic."

"You already have."

"He's right, Aaron. You did it at game this evening." Mags corrected.

I wasn't sure how to feel about any of this. On one hand the concept of magic was freaking awesome. On the other, there was no way I was ready for something as heavy as this. I was a kid. I wanted to be a kid. Magic and adventure were things I only dreamed about. Now that they were seemingly a reality, I wasn't sure I wanted them.

"On the night of a witch or wizard's thirteenth birthday, he or she will come into their power. There is no hiding from or delaying it. It happens to each of us. This is why I sent your parents away.

"Most go relatively unnoticed until their transition is complete, but when you visited me earlier today I could feel how strong you were becoming. I've no doubt others noticed it as well. This has inadvertently drawn the attention of those whom would see your ability toward their own ends. I could not, in good conscious, allow you to face it alone and unsupervised."

"You're saying you made all of this happen?"

"No. I'm saying it was going to happen one way or another. Having felt how powerful you're to become, I didn't want you to have to experience it alone."

It was more than I was able to understand and yet I could feel that he was holding back. I wanted to go home and forget any of this had ever happened. I knew that that was impossible. A bell cannot be unrung. Whatever was happening would find me no matter where I went or how far I ran. "Why me?"

Grandpa shrugged. "Why does the caterpillar become a butterfly? It's in your blood. My grandfather had it. As did his before him. But if you're asking if you're somehow special, aside from being born to a magical family, the answer is no. There is no hidden prophecy or 'chosen one' aspect to your existence. At least none that I'm aware of.

"Some people are just naturally stronger than others. And when one arises there are always those who seek to manipulate them. That's the danger you find yourself in. Until you've claimed your mantle and learned to harness your abilities with control there will be many who will seek to use you. It's my intention to prevent that."

"So you're like a good wizard. You're gonna protect him?" Raj asked. The look on his face told me he was following the story far better than I. At least someone was. I was still stuck on the 'magic is real' part.

"What do we do now?" Mags joined in. I'd never seen her look so concerned. Whether she was willing to admit it or not, her tone suggested she was worried about me.

"Strictly speaking, a wizard's first trial is a sacred event. One which I am forbidden to interfere in, as are all wizards. Though that will not stop them from using any means of influence at their disposal. It is up to Aaron to find his own way. He is to become what he is to become. I can offer no more than tutelage and insight. Even the protections of my tower are muted until his path is chosen.

"I've already petitioned the Council of Nine. It's my hope they'll see his potential and grant sanctuary. Such a ruling will protect him until he's mastered his power."

"What if they don't?" Flickering firelight danced across Mags' face. I couldn't help but notice how pretty she was in that moment. Even with the worry she wore, she was so beautiful. She had reason to worry.

Everything that was happening was beyond my control. I was a pawn in someone else's game. I was trapped in something I didn't understand. Even my grandpa, by his own admission, had an agenda. He may not seek to use me as he claimed others intended, but he had purpose for my power. I could feel it.

"If sanctuary is denied we have but one course remaining. We must hold out until he learns to protect himself. Only then will outside influences be unable to manipulate him."

# Chapter 7
## Mystical Montage

I'd love to say the next few hours raced by like some dubbed training montage where I learned everything I needed to know over the course of a single upbeat song. Instead, I spent my time studying stuff I couldn't hope to understand.

Grandpa lectured on the positions of constellations, the season and time of year, temperature, weather, and so much more. He explained how all these things had an impact on the fabrication and weaving of spells. He told me, with rather long and tedious explanations and examples, how I would have to account for all these factors to truly understand the slightest use of magic.

All I really noticed was the thunderous tick of a nearby grand clock as it rattled out the passing seconds. I felt like I was in school again, waiting for class to be over so I could hang out with my friends.

I hadn't seen Mags or Raj in quite some time, though I kept glancing around in hopes of spotting one or the other.

Mags had disappeared down a fire lit room to my right. The bricked walls were lined with suits of armor and archaic weaponry that rested on stands here and there. It looked like some kind of medieval museum.

There was no telling where Raj had disappeared. He was fascinated by literally everything. I hadn't seen him stay in the same place for more than a few minutes since we'd arrived.

I sat in the center of a massive training room, as grandpa called it. It was more like a gathering of three long and narrow rooms that were laid atop one another at different angles to form a six-legged star.

Towering columns stood where the walls met and stone arches, scrawled in symbols, stretched over each wing's entrance. The symbols were supposed to tell me each area's purpose, but so far all I'd deciphered was some kind of warning about great power having great responsibility.

I learned more about the various wings by what they contained than by the odd writings labeling them. For instance, the room behind me was fairly intimidating with hundreds of flying sparks of varying sizes that darted this way and that. Grandpa warned us not to go in there. He said it was some kind of defensive training area and that none of us were prepared to attempt such a thing.

The central area, where I'd spent much of my time, was a rather large room unto itself. Each corner column contained a door that led into other parts of the tower. There were freestanding bookshelves in one quarter, tables and chairs in another, and various other odds and ends which didn't help the school vibe I was getting.

The glass ceiling over the central area was domed and made of what I guessed to be some kind of magnifying telescope. I could study not only the location but the actual surfaces of individual planets and stars with the naked eye.

The other wings were filled with numerous devices and purposes. One appeared to have a ringed pit which had two metal dummies fighting each other with swords. Another housed what looked to be an obstacle course. Grandpa assured me none of it was lethal but he amended by casually stating, 'You'd be surprised what you can live through.'

I caught sight of Mags out the corner of my eye. I couldn't be certain due to the low light and the distance but it looked like she was wearing pieces of a golden suit of armor. I turned but she was gone before I could get a better look.

"Aaron, pay attention!" Grandpa snapped for what had to have been the thousandth time.

That was the one thing I was learning. The concept of time meant nothing to a wizard. I have no idea how long I'd been studying all this stuff. It could have been hours, maybe even weeks. Time seemed to stand still and rush simultaneously. The clock however suggested it had only been about half an hour since we'd arrived.

I spotted Mags again. Sure enough, she had on a pair of shoulder pauldrons and gauntlets. We locked eyes and the sight of her smile nearly made me blush. Fortunately, she was gone again before I could stop it.

"Aaron!"

I felt it before I saw it. A bolt of crackling red energy crashed through the shield I'd been attempting. I felt it crumble into pieces and dissipate, the energy evaporating with it.

"You must keep your focus at all times. A wizard who drops his guard is a wizard who dies. The shield will hold only so long as your resolve remains intact."

"Come on, Grandpa. We've been at this for hours. How much do you expect me to remember without a break?"

"Time is meaningless. It bends to *your* will. You do not cater to *it*!"

A heavy sigh escaped me and I set my feet once again. Drawing on the twisting feeling in my gut, I pulled at the white flicks of light in the air. They slowly started to come together, locking into a large disc that floated in front of me. No sooner than the final piece fell into place the entire thing flashed and became invisible. I honestly don't know if I could see it, or if I was simply feeling it so strongly that I knew where it was. Either way, my shield was still there and ready for action.

"Ready?"

"Yeah."

A solid blast slammed into me and I slid backward nearly six inches. Sparks showered around me, but rather than exploding outward, they sucked into one another and faded away. I could feel numerous cracks in my shield. Another blast like that one and I feared it would collapse.

A barrage of smaller energy bolts shot from Grandpa's fingers, imploding against the shield, fracturing it further. The flashes of light were beautiful to look upon, reminding me of some of the fireworks I'd seen last summer.

Sweat beaded on my forehead as I strained to keep my focus. It took everything I had to hold the protective barrier together. Seeing the last of the bolts dissipate, I lowered my arms. "Why do the sparks do that?"

"Do what?"

"Pull together and fizzle out. Why don't they explode into a big blast like you see on TV? I'd imagine a big explosion would do more damage than these little sparks you keep throwing at me."

A smirk appeared on grandpa's lips but it was gone an instant later. "Much of what we do is done from the shadows. The last time magic was known to the mundane world, our kind was hunted to near extinction. If we were to create such catastrophic destruction without reasonable explanation, questions would form quicker than the greatest among us could fabricate answers. It's much safer to make any magics you wield appear as close to natural occurrence as possible.

"Moreover, the civilian population is protected from our abilities. It's part of the price which hides us from public scrutiny."

"What price?"

"How did you feel earlier this evening when you discovered the reality of magic?"

"Um—I guess I was pretty confused. I thought Raj was pulling a prank on me."

"Would it be a fair assessment to say you struggled with your sanity?"

"I guess that's one way to put it."

"The existence of magic must be safeguarded. If you were to use your magic in plain view of a regular human, the insanity they would suffer from such a display would loop back on you. This is why most of the wizards throughout history who interacted with man were believed insane. Their power doubled back on them and drove them to such. You must always consider who may be watching, Aaron. Even an accidental display can have drastic consequences."

"But what about Mags and Raj? They witnessed magic and they haven't gone insane."

"I'm uncertain as to why they're able to perceive such things. There have always been a few who are sensitive to the arcane. It's likely this trait is what drew them to your side in the first place."

Another blast caught me off guard. I narrowly pulled a shield together before it hit. It shattered into pieces which evaporated as they fell. I landed on my butt and glared up at Grandpa with distain. "How am I supposed to stay focused when balls of light keep flying at my face? I can only absorb so many before the shield breaks!"

"You must learn focus. It doesn't matter if your clothing is aflame, you're falling from a great height, or if the world is falling apart around you. No matter what, you have to keep calm and approach every situation with a clear mind. Nothing beneficial comes from anger or other strong emotions. It clouds the mind. Likewise, fear holds you back. It serves to keep you alive by lying to you. Learn to silence your emotions and you'll master every task you set out to accomplish."

"This is stupid. Why do I have to learn how to make a shield? Why can't I be the one attacking?"

"If you think you can, by all means." Grandpa showed me his palms, opening himself to attack. It felt more like a taunt than anything.

Picking myself off the floor, I planted my feet and tried to summon the energies like he showed me. That seemed to be the base element of every spell, though the source of those energies seemed to come from different places. This felt more like bits of static electricity hovering in the air around me. I pulled as many as I could find into a small ball of crackling energy. It tingled against my flesh but didn't hurt. I kept pulling, soaking up as much static as I could find but I couldn't seem to make anything larger than a golf ball.

"Are you going to cast, or wait until I die of old age?" Grandpa taunted with a smile.

My entire body began to shake. I was struggling to contain the minute amount of power I'd collected. It was now or never. If I didn't get rid of it I knew it was going to start shocking me.

Clearing my head, I drew back and thrust both palms outward, willing the underwhelming energy ball toward Grandpa. It launched with the enthusiasm of a lead balloon and began to fizzle no sooner than it hit the ground.

I stared helplessly as the little ball of sparks rolled across the floor. I could tell Grandpa was trying not to laugh, to which I was glad. I wasn't sure I could handle being laughed at right now.

"Hey, A-A-Ron, look at this!" Raj came running from a corridor to my left. I knew it was a mistake the moment I made it. I turned to look at him.

Out the corner of my eye, I could see my minuscule lightning ball. The moment it reached Grandpa it struck a shimmering golden field that encompassed him entirely. I'm not completely sure what happened but somehow my micro bolt became supercharged and flung back at me with a speed not even Grandpa's strongest attack had had.

I tried to bring a shield up but the particles couldn't get there in time. I could taste the air. A throbbing pain coursed through my body. When my vision cleared I found myself staring at the constellations through the glass ceiling. Grandpa, Mags, and Raj were standing over me.

"Are you okay?" Mags asked, kneeling to help me up.

"No!" Grandpa reached out and grabbed her arm before she could touch me. "He's still charged. He'll be fine in a few minutes but he has to ground first."

"Looks to me like he was already grounded." Raj laughed, shaking his head. "Anyway, watch this!" He extended his hands, wrapped in a pair of simple looking leather gloves.

I couldn't see what he was going on about but Mags let out a gasp of shock. "What? What's happening?"

"Look." Raj ordered, nodding the direction he'd come.

I half rolled, straining to find whatever it was I was supposed to see. When I did, I wanted to punch him.

After all the effort I'd put in to controlling the tiniest bit of magic, Raj was making a pair of swords fight each other without so much as a bead of sweat. I turned away in disgust.

"Did you see?"

"Yeah, I saw!" I tried to sit up but my body wasn't having it. I could still feel the electricity coursing through me and I wondered how much longer I'd have to wait.

"Young man, I've asked you repeatedly to leave things alone. Yet again, here you are with one of my many prized possessions, playing with something you don't understand. Any number of items you'll find within this tower can break you in ways you can't begin to imagine. Now please, return the gloves to where you found them and leave my belongings alone."

I heard the swords clank to the floor and the joy that was so often visible on Raj's face had suddenly faded. His head drooped and he solemnly started walking away.

"Don't you think that was a little mean? He's just trying to make sense of all of this in the only way he knows how." Mags defended. It was the first time I'd heard her stand up for Raj. Still, I could understand Grandpa's side. Raj had a habit of getting too comfortable no matter where he was. He'd done the same thing with my stuff on many occasions.

I twisted and got to my stomach. I was tired of lying on the ground and it didn't appear anyone, other than Mags maybe, was going to help me up.

Lightning crackled and sparked and danced with each movement. No sooner than my bare hand touched the floor, I found myself wishing I'd found another way.

All the electricity that had taken root suddenly shot out in a rush. I collapsed face first onto the stone.

I could hear Mags somewhere in the distance. "Is he all right?"

I could feel her nearing. She knelt along my left side and reached down, her hand inches away.

"He's safe to touch. The energy exited him all at once. It's going to leave him weak for a little while but he'll be okay."

I wish I could have gotten up. I was still awake but my body refused to respond. I didn't have the strength to perform the simplest task.

Grandpa's casual tone made me want to hit him. Truth be told, I was feeling the urge to hit a lot of people lately. That wasn't something I usually felt the desire to do.

I felt Mags touch me and a strange revitalizing comfort took hold. I couldn't see it but I could feel it. It was as if a golden glow radiated from her touch and spread throughout my entire body. The longer she remained in contact, the better I felt.

I don't know how long I laid there but eventually my body started to obey. Slowly, I picked myself up and got to my feet.

"Thank you." My voice was little more than a whisper.

Mags smiled in appreciation and stepped back.

I don't know why the urge hit me, but I knew this was the only chance I was going to get. Grandpa had been prepared the last time.

I drew in energies as quick and discrete as possible, collecting them into a concentrated ball. If Grandpa noticed, he didn't let on.

Feeling the energy bolt was as large as I could make it, I launched it at its target. It closed the short distance in the blink of an eye.

As before, the glimmering shield surrounding Grandpa shimmered and my spell fired back at me. I was ready this time. I summoned my own shield, pulling the puzzle of pieces together faster than I ever had before. They flew into place and locked together. The white haze solidified, though something happened then I hadn't expected.

My shield turned gold, like Grandpa's, and the spell hit. It swarmed around me, looking for any crack in my defenses. Unable to find one, it recollected with itself and shot out a second time.

Grandpa extended his hand, hastily constructing a disc shield. The bolt of energy smashed into it and imploded.

As the sparks faded away his intense gaze settled on me. I watched a smile creep into its place. "Well done, lad. I knew you could both attack and defend. You just needed the proper motivations."

I suddenly understood something he'd been trying to teach me. Manipulation was the way of a wizard. I'd grown up with it. The praise, the tests, the way of thinking—It was all manipulation. He'd been manipulating me my entire life.

I felt betrayed on so many levels. My parents forgetting my birthday and leaving for their trip. Grandpa coming over to watch me. The existence of magic. My place in it. And now, with my first successful spell. I'd been played since birth. I wasn't sure I was willing to be played any more.

Before I could put much thought into my feelings, a strange sensation tingled down my spine.

An alarm sounded. Vibrations echoed from somewhere deep in the tower. The floor and walls shook, though I heard the voice in my head as much as I felt it in my surroundings.

"Wizard Giles Corey, The Council of Nine accepts your petition to meet in regard to the novice, Aaron Corey, and his associates. A carriage awaits your occupancy."

"Time to go." Grandpa stated casually, suddenly wearing a set of elegant white robes that weren't there a moment earlier.

"What? Where are we going? I thought you said we'd be safe here? Why are we leaving?" Mags asked.

"Didn't you hear?"

"Hear what?" I could see the growing confusion on her face.

"The council thing Grandpa told us about is ready." I replied, surprised she hadn't heard the message. I don't know how anyone could have missed it, but since Grandpa had clearly heard it too, maybe it was a wizard thing.

"Where's the other boy?" Grandpa asked, looking around.

"I'm here." Raj announced, appearing from the corridor to our left. He had a guilty look on his face and I suspected he was up to something. Before I could say anything, Grandpa directed us toward one of the column embedded doors.

I know for a fact we walked through the same door we'd entered from earlier, but instead of finding a staircase, we were greeted by the cool night air on the landing.

I almost didn't see it. In fact, had it not been for the void of distant stars I wouldn't have.

A pitched black coach with two equally black horses rested at the far edge of the landing. It wasn't until we were nearly on top of it before I realized it was accentuated in silver. A nine-headed hydra, also in silver, embossed the side door with each head staring at us. It's snaking body wrapped the side of the carriage to form what I recognized as a protective ward.

The horses were easily the largest I'd ever seen. They were nearly twice as tall as the few I'd been around and had long glistening fur that sprouted just below their knees to run down over their hooves.

I had to do a double take. Instead of leather straps and bridle, thin wisps of swirling energy ran from both horses, tethering them to the front of the carriage and into the hands of the silent coachman. He didn't bother to acknowledge us as we neared.

Grandpa stepped forward and spoke just over a whisper.

Despite my best effort I couldn't hear what he said. I suspected it was some kind of password or something because the carriage doors split down the middle and swung outward to reveal an intricate set of curved steps that led into the decorative coach.

Mags and Raj were the first to enter. Grandpa stepped in front of me before I could follow.

"Aaron, I urge you to use caution when we meet the council. They're not forgiving of fools nor are they a patient sort. Speak only when addressed directly and be sure to think beforehand. I don't know if you've uncovered the importance of this meeting but I assure you if they turn their backs it's going to be a dire evening for us all."

"I understand." I didn't but I thought saying it would help.

Grandpa nodded once and stepped aside, allowing me to join my friends.

The Wizard's Grandson

Levi Samuel

# Chapter 8
## Sanctuary

The coach interior caught me by surprise. I hadn't noticed it from the steps. In fact, its grandeur hadn't set in until I'd already crossed the threshold and fully immersed myself. This wasn't a carriage. It was something far greater.

I couldn't help but think of one of my favorite TV shows. The TARDIS was always bigger on the inside. Though this thing clearly wasn't some police-box time-machine, and I certainly wouldn't consider my grandpa the Doctor. Even still, what I found inside was one of the most impressive displays I'd ever seen.

I stood just inside a free floating opening to the outside world where Grandpa was coming through. We seemed to be near the center of what I could only describe as a grand ballroom.

There were no ornate benches or plump cushions. There were no wall mounted screens or windows to be seen. Not even the distant walls were visible from where I stood, being shrouded in a strange glowing fog.

Instead, a huge glistening chandelier dangled overhead, casting flickers of ethereal light about the place. A massive table spanned the center of the room, loaded to capacity with fruits, meats, breads, bowls of candy, and just about every other amenity I'd ever desired. I'd never considered what a feast would look like but the sight before me solidified my understanding of the term.

Raj wasted no time. He had a plate piled two fists high and his mouth equally full before my initial shock had even worn off. It wasn't until he'd swallowed that first massive mouthful that he finally found a seat.

That was one of the things that caught me off guard. There were only four chairs, each one wooden and carved with strange designs that spoke to me. I have no way of explaining how I knew what they said but I could feel they were meant for us.

I glanced to Mags who looked just as uncertain as I felt. She cautiously pulled out the chair I knew was hers and took a seat.

A reassuring nod from Grandpa told me it was okay. "The council provides both comfort and safety during our journey. Eat your fill and get some rest while you can. There's no telling when such a luxury may come again."

I pulled out my chair, feeling the pattern of carvings beneath my fingers. There was a conflicted texture forming the design, like it didn't know what it wanted to be, or more aptly, like it had the potential to be anything it wanted if only it'd make a choice. I released the chair and plopped down beside Raj.

Mags sat across the table from us and timidly reached for a platter of fried chicken.

If it hadn't been for everything else that had happened this night, I would have felt like we'd just been assigned to Gryffindor and were enjoying our first meal at Hogwarts. As it were, this wasn't Hogwarts, and as much as we were experiencing a new world, a world of magic, this felt far more dangerous.

I couldn't believe how much black there was. The table cloth, the napkins, the plates, even the goblets were so dark it seemed all the light was being absorbed into them. Were it not for the veins of silver running through the void it would have been uncomfortable to look upon. Even the floor was made of a black and silver granite.

Cautiously, I reached out and grabbed a silver ladle, helping myself to what looked like a pot of mashed potatoes. In no time I had what I judged to be a decent meal before me. It was the pile of spicy chips, cheese sauce, and gummy bears that really set it apart from an ordinary dinner.

"Where are the drinks?" Raj asked, goblet in hand as he searched the table.

"What would you like?" Grandpa replied.

"Dr. Pepper. But I'm not seeing—Wait! How? Oh, that's awesome!"

I glanced over to see what he was so excited about. To all of our surprise, except for Grandpa it seemed, his goblet had filled itself with a dark fizzy liquid. I watched him cautiously take a sip.

"Holy crap. That is Dr. Pepper!" He took a big gulp and I saw the ideas forming.

Grandpa must have suspected the same, since he spoke before Raj could open his mouth.

"The goblets can produce any liquid you desire, though for obvious reasons certain liquids are restricted by age."

"That sucks! Can't someone like A-A-Ron trick the cup into thinking he's older?"

"Sure." Grandpa replied.

"Really?"

"Yes. It's quite a simple cantrip for one who's mastered their abilities and learned to augment spells."

"How long will that take?"

I was curious myself but it was easier to let Raj ask the questions.

A mild smirk appeared on Grandpa's lips. "With steady practice and an uncanny ability to learn quickly, he'll probably reach Master status within twenty years."

Raj stared blankly, his refilled cup an inch from his lips. "Twenty years? But—but by then he won't need to trick the cup."

"Exactly."

Sometime during the revelry of food, drink, and conversation, the room shifted without our notice. The walls were much closer and the table seemed smaller. A short distance away, a fireplace burned gently, though I can't be certain in which wall it sat, or even which direction it faced. It always seemed to be in front of me no matter what.

I hadn't realized how chilly it was getting until I felt the flame fight the cold back and take dominion over the room.

At some point our carved wooden chairs shifted into more comfortable versions. Raj lounged in a giant red beanbag. I knew it had to be the same wooden chair as it still had the depictions I knew were meant for him.

Mags rested lengthwise on a couch that was just wide enough for her. She was intently studying the fireplace.

Grandpa had kicked back in a blue recliner and was snoring lightly.

And my chair—well—it remained the same hard wooden chair it had been at dinner, seemingly waiting for me to tell it what to do.

The walls were closer than ever. For the first time I noticed dark curtains hanging over tall narrow windows.

I finished my drink, which had been eerily close to the sweet tea my grandma used to make, and wiped my mouth. Getting to my feet I approached the nearest curtain and pulled it aside.

I knew it had to be an illusion of some kind. The view was completely wrong. While it was getting cold, it hadn't been anywhere near cold enough for snow to form, let alone to accumulate the several inches that rested on the ground far below us. Moreover, the retirement home, while large, even beyond the walls that hid its true visage, was nowhere near as grand as the spanning city beneath us. Not even all of Fremont Hills and its surrounding cities was as large as what I saw. If the sight was to be believed, this was some kind of huge metropolitan in a place I'd never been before.

"Where do you think we're going?" Raj asked through a mouthful of food, standing suddenly beside me. I hadn't heard him get up.

"I don't know. I guess wherever the Council of Nine is. It doesn't look like any place I've been before, but I don't think we can be too far from home. I don't think so anyway. Honestly, I don't know much of anything anymore. For all I know we went through some kind of portal and are on the other side of the world right now."

I felt Mags before I knew she was standing there, but I jumped all the same when her hand wrapped around mine. It took everything I had to keep from blushing. I turned to look into her deep green eyes. All things considered she was holding it together quite well, though I couldn't blame her for being freaked out. I was freaked out too.

A mild tremor shook the ground beneath us. I stole a final glance out the window, discovering we'd landed. I closed the curtain and turned away. It was then I realized the room had fully vanished and we were in a regular black and silver carriage with benches along the walls and a single door opposite from where we stood.

Grandpa sat up and twisted to his feet. Turning to face us he gave a stern yet friendly expression. "I need the three of you to be on your best behavior. The council is divided. I do not know if this will end in our favor or against it, but I can tell you we need to be extremely careful. Do not wander. Do not speak unless spoken to, and only if I nod approval. They're likely to make us wait for some time. I understand this will be considered boring to some of you but you must be patient. If we do not explore this avenue there's no telling when or even if the hunt for Aaron will end."

"Wait! The hunt? What hunt? Who's hunting me?" Was this the first time I was hearing about this? How could I miss such a detail? That raised the importance of everything to a level greater than I was prepared for.

"There's no telling who's involved but we need to exercise caution on all fronts. More than the shadow is likely to take an interest in you. If employed, you could tilt the scales toward either favor. That makes you a weapon for both sides."

Mags squeezed my hand, silently telling me more than words could say. Then, sooner than I was ready, she released and walked toward the door where my grandpa was waiting.

I sighed and started after her. How could everything get so complicated in such a short time? All I wanted was to have my birthday party and hang out with my friends. Now it seemed the very fate of my survival was hanging in the balance.

"Think of it this way—" Raj added. "—at least we don't have to go back to school on Monday." He smiled before tossing one of the numerous items he'd pilfered into his mouth. A part of me suspected the table had disappeared just to keep Raj from eating everything.

I followed Mags out the door and onto a glossy cobblestone street at the base of a round dais. Snow was piled atop everything except this small section of road and a single pathway which led up the stone steps to a set of towering red doors that arched at their peak.

The doors were set into a stone frame that adjoined what I could only describe as a castle. It might have been a cathedral or some other similar structure. I wasn't totally fluent in medieval architecture terms. All I knew was this was easily the biggest building I'd ever seen and I felt dwarfed in its shadow.

"Remember my words." Grandpa gave each of us a final look and started up the melted path.

By the time we reached the top I was nearly out of breath. I should have counted the steps but I didn't. All I can say is there were a lot.

Two guards stood to each side of the towering red doors. They were dressed in metal plate armor and held polished halberds mirrored as if in anticipation of threat. Silver and jeweled swords were sheathed on each of their left hips.

Were I anywhere else I would have thought they looked out of place but the sheer majesty of everything around me made these *knights* look fitting.

Grandpa came to a stop a few steps from the door. "Giles Corey and company here to seek audience with the council."

The guards showed no acknowledgment of his presence. To my surprise, the doors began to creak open.

I'd never been in a castle before but the smell was exactly how I imagined it—musky and stale, kind of like moist dirt. There was an odd temperature to the air exiting the growing crack. It was warm yet chilling at the same time, like the mouth of a cave in the middle of winter.

Orange light flickered off the stone floor casting away the shadows that clung to every surface. As the doors came to a halt they echoed out a timed crash, standing fully opened and awaiting our entry.

Grandpa signaled for us to wait.

Footsteps echoed from somewhere inside the fire lit halls but I couldn't immediately see to whom they belonged. After a lingering moment a dark silhouette with a long shadow formed in the distance and started to move toward us.

In mere seconds, a tall man wrapped in a heavy gray cloak stood just behind the threshold. His arms were concealed beneath the garment and a hood obscured his face, though I could just see the edge of white hair peeking out at the sides.

"Giles, my old friend, how are you?" The man dropped his hood and a gloved hand appeared between the overlapped cloth.

In my opinion he was extremely well dressed for someone wearing a cloak. It wasn't quite the formal attire my dad had worn to some of the events he and my mom attended, but it was certainly formal in another era. I'd seen similar clothing worn on stage when my parents took me to see Hamlet. I found it quite silly looking at the time but now, in this place, it seemed to fit.

"It's good to see you, Gerald. I didn't know you'd gone to work for these stiffs."

"Times are hard. We can't all afford to retire and live in such luxury." The man, apparently named Gerald, laughed and released his grip on my grandpa's hand. "I hear you've asked for council with the nine."

"Yeah. The boy here—" Grandpa gestured to me. "—hit his thirteenth this evening and we're hoping they'll end open season on him."

Gerald let out a doubtful sigh. "Well, come on in. Best not keep em waiting. I don't know how well you'll fair though. The council hasn't been overly forthcoming with assistance to most of late."

Grandpa waved dismissively and ushered us through the doors which began to close the moment we were through. "I'm not too concerned. I've got an ace in the hole. Five to be exact."

"I see."

Grandpa and Gerald continued talking as we made our way through the castle. I stopped paying attention pretty soon after we got inside. It was more reminiscence of the old days and what they'd been up to since they last spoke. I didn't see any need to listen to that.

Beyond the entrance corridor it opened into a grand hall. There were stairs to the right and a pillared entrance straight ahead. Voices could be heard from both directions and I had no idea which way we needed to go. Fortunately, Gerald seemed to be on top of it. He turned right and we started up the stairs.

My thoughts about what this place might be were completely changed the moment we reached the top. I'd expected some kind of stuffy structured gathering with a bunch of old dudes who approached the world from the philosophy that things could only be one particular way and all other ways were wrong. I wasn't entirely convinced that's not how things were, but I was surprised to find hundreds of kids all around us.

They were everywhere. Boys, girls, young, old, and all dressed in similar outfits. This was some kind of school if ever I'd seen one.

I felt like all eyes were on me as we made our way through the crowded corridors. What was more confusing though, if this was one of those fancy schools where people slept in dorms, they should have been in bed hours ago.

Gerald turned left at the top of the stairs and led us through the throng of people filling what I imagined to be the main hall. To the right there were multiple openings into a room with several large tables. It looked to be a dining hall. There was another set of stairs with a balcony behind us, and straight ahead another pillared divide into a narrow corridor.

The presence of guards standing at either side of the entrance wasn't lost on me.

"What do you think they're doing here?" Raj asked, eyeing the kids who were likewise looking at us.

"Looks like a school of some kind." Mags responded, clearly thinking the same thing I was.

"What kind of school runs in the middle of the night? No place I'd want to go." Raj added.

"I was just thinking about that. It's got to be around midnight or later. Maybe we went further than we thought. Or maybe it's like Grandpa was telling me earlier. Time doesn't mean anything to a wizard."

"I told you he was a bright one." Grandpa nudged Gerald, but it got my attention and I felt my cheeks flush red with embarrassment. I wasn't one for receiving compliments.

"He'd better be if you hope to pull this off. I personally think you're tipping your hand."

We stepped into another hallway between two guards and emerged at an intersection. It ran left and right and two sets of wide doors sat in the wall directly ahead of us.

"Go on in. I'll inform them you've arrived."

"Thanks, my friend. Until we meet again." Grandpa did a weird bow with a hand flourish only to have it returned by his friend. As soon as Gerald was gone, Grandpa twisted the knob and pushed one of the heavy wooden doors open.

Inside felt overly formal. An old couch rested between the two sets of doors. A wide cabinet, worn with age took up an entire side wall and the other was filled by a pair of leather wrapped chairs and a book filled shelf between them. The wall ahead had a single set of double doors at its center. Even from the entrance I could see the glowing strands of magic sealing them.

"And now we wait." Grandpa took a seat in one of the leather chairs.

Mags, Raj, and myself sat on the couch.

Before I could get comfortable a loud knock echoed from the other side of the magically sealed door and I watched the enchantment unwrap and fall away.

Grandpa got to his feet and signaled me to join him. "You two stay put. We'll be back in a few minutes."

Just as I reached Grandpa's side the doors flew open and I found myself staring into a large round chamber. Shadow and fog obscured everything within. I could just barely make out the man in front of us.

He was shorter than I expected, standing just a few inches taller than I. Most others I'd encountered of late seemed to be towering by comparison, but that didn't make this man any less intimidating. He wore gray robes similar in design to the white ones around Grandpa, but this guy had a sword strapped to his hip and a nasty looking scar that ran from his jaw, across his nose, and ended at his forehead.

"Who comes here?"

"Giles Corey, Wizard of the Third Order and Master of the White Arts, Retired, along with novice wizard, Aaron Corey."

"And what be your intention for this audience."

"I seek sanctuary for the novice until such a time as he masters his ability and can maintain such status for himself."

"Does he possess an arcanum?"

"He does."

"Has he bound said arcanum?"

"He has not."

"Very well. I shall inform the council. Wait until such a time as you are summoned again."

The man took a step back, closed the doors, and knocked a second time, reactivating the magical seal.

"What was that all about?" Raj asked.

"Formality. That's why I asked you to remain quiet unless directly addressed. Any break in protocol can result in delay, dismissal, or offense. We cannot afford any of them at this time."

I started to return to my seat but Grandpa grabbed my shoulder and stopped me in my tracks.

"They won't be long. Best to simply wait here."

As if he knew what was happening on the other side of the door, another knock echoed and the door opened again. The man reappeared and peered down at me. "The council accepts your petition and is ready to meet."

He spun on his heel, took three steps inside, turned left, and spun again, inviting us to enter.

Grandpa led me to the man's side where we stopped until he closed and resealed the door.

The room was much larger than I'd initially thought, though that didn't mean I had room to explore. Truth was, there wasn't anything to explore.

A singular narrow walkway led from the door to a central circular pedestal. Everything beyond lacked any kind of floor so far as I could tell. If it had a bottom, I couldn't see it. A tall curved wall sprouted from the darkness on the outer ring. I could narrowly make out the nine towering thrones resting atop, but from where I stood I couldn't see anyone sitting in them.

The doorman took the lead and guided us to our perspective positions at the center of the platform. He summoned a staff out of thin air and slammed its base onto the granite floor. A thunderous clap echoed and flame erupted from the basins mounted on the outer walls. It seemed to dispel much of the fog and shadow and I suddenly realized why I couldn't see the council. Their chairs were empty.

"Retired Wizard of the Third Order and Master of the White Arts, Giles Corey and novice wizard, Aaron Corey seek audience with the Council of the Nine!"

I felt the ground shake with his rap and the echo of his voice sent chills down my spine. I could feel a tingle in the air and the little sparks Grandpa had been teaching me to look out for began to gather about each of the nine seats.

Almost in unison people began to appear, seated and dressed in familiar robes. Three wore white, three wore gray, and three wore black.

No sooner than the council presented themselves, the doorman offered the same salute I'd seen Grandpa and Gerald exchange. Then, he turned and disappeared into shadow, though I suspect he was still somewhere close.

"Giles Corey, by what rite or benefit do you expect to gain the favor of this council?" One of the black robes asked, though I wasn't certain which one.

"By rite of my status as a magician of the ancient arts, and benefit to uphold the sacred oath each of us has taken at one time or another to not interfere with the balance by manipulation of those undereducated."

"And how may we know that this novice has not already been indoctrinated by such manipulations of your own?"

"By way of a test. Today is his awakening and I don't have to explain to you the threat of the power radiating from him."

"And how do you believe we should test him?" One of the white wizards responded.

"Enrollment."

I heard a few of them scoff at the idea though I didn't have a clue what they were talking about. They may as well have been speaking in riddles.

"Do you think we open our doors for just any novice who happens to wander in?" One of the blacks retorted.

"I do not. However, some of you may recall that I am an alumnus of this institution for higher learning. This novice, being of my lineage, is entitled to admission standards under legacy guideline article two-eighteen, section twenty-three."

"I'm aware of your record here, Wizard Corey. As I'm also aware of your contributions. However, I would point out that section twenty-five of the same article to which you refer states, any legacy must first bond their arcanum before the enrollment process can begin. Am I correct in the understanding that the novice has not yet bonded his arcanum?" One of the whites asked.

"You are. However, I urge you to overlook this small detail as his life is in jeopardy. He hasn't had the opportunity to bond on account of outside influences seeking what is his."

"Wizard Corey, how are we to know this to be true?" One of the blacks replied. "For all we know this story of pursuit is some fabrication in order to elicit an emotional response and grant early enrollment, and sanctuary by extension. I'm of the opinion this novice does not belong if he's unable to perform so simple a task as bonding his arcanum."

"Aleister, you and I have never seen eye to eye but you know better than to accuse me of laying falsehoods, especially under the watch of the council."

"Let us hear what the novice has to say on his own behalf." The black robed wizard known as Aleister retorted.

Grandpa glanced at me and nodded, giving me permission to speak.

I didn't know what they wanted me to say. Truthfully, I wasn't sure what any of this was about and I didn't want to say the wrong thing from a misunderstanding. "Um, can you repeat the question?"

"Do you feel your life is in danger?" One of the grays prompted.

"I—um—well, I don't know what's out there but I've had a bunch of stuff following me lately. It doesn't seem to matter how fast I run or where I go, it's always right there."

"What's right there?" One of the whites asked.

"I don't know. It's always hidden in darkness. Even when it's supposed to be light out. I haven't seen exactly what it is but it's always there, waiting to get me."

"Absurd! Why would anything or anyone want to snatch a young boy such as yourself? It's preposterous!" Aleister proclaimed.

I was starting to get mad. This guy was accusing me of lying. He didn't even know me. "I'm not lying!"

"Of course you're not." Aleister said sarcastically. "And just how much has your grandfather coached you in this story? Surely he told you to throw in some tears for good measure."

"He hasn't told me to say anything. It really happened. A few times. It happened when I was coming home. And again when I was outside my front door. Then again when I accidently teleported."

"Excuse me, you teleported? I thought you hadn't bonded yet?" One of the females in white interjected.

"Yeah. I was playing a game with my friends and I accidently teleported to the patch of woods just outside my grandpa's retirement home."

"He was reading from his arcanum and accidently activated one of the spells." Grandpa added.

"Amazing! Yet, I'm curious as to how he was able to read it if he hasn't bonded yet." The white woman continued.

"It just goes to show how powerful he has the potential to become. Possibly more so under this council's tutelage."

I was starting to understand what Grandpa was pushing for and I wasn't sure I liked it one bit. "Wait, are you trying to get me to go to school here?"

"Yes. Here you'll have everything you need to learn to control your power. And by being enrolled you'll have sanctuary from anything and everything that might seek to use you." Grandpa answered as if I already knew all of this.

"No! I don't want to go to school here. I already have a school."

"Your school cannot teach you how to protect yourself."

"But my friends are there. I can't just leave them."

"It sounds like the boy's made up his mind." Aleister said coolly.

"Giles, won't you and the boy wait outside while the council convenes on this matter. We'll call you when we've made a decision." The white robed woman suggested.

The door man reappeared and guided us back to the door from which we'd come.

# Chapter 9
## The Appeal

I was happy to have some time in the small room. It seemed Grandpa and I had some things to discuss and I needed to get it through his head that I wasn't going to change schools. I had things the way I liked them and I wasn't about to let him change it simply because he thought he knew what was best for me.

"I'm not leaving my school. All my friends are there and I'm not leaving!" I demanded, turning to face Grandpa.

"Aaron—" He started with a soft tone, kneeling in front of me. "—I fear you don't understand the danger you're in. Being a magician isn't all daffodils and rainbows. There are forces at play which would see you enslaved for the rest of your natural born life. Others would have you beheaded or burned at the stake for simply being who you are. The world in which we exist is an imperfect place. That's why we're here. We bring balance. The council itself, as flawed as their ideologies can be at times, is balanced. Three white, three black, three gray; the good, the bad, and the in-between working in harmony to maintain balance."

"That's dumb. You can't have balance with an odd number!"

"True. But perfect balance in all regards becomes stagnant. That's why the gray wizards exist. They play the middle ground, tilting the scales between light and dark, maintaining a steady fluctuation between the two."

"I'm still not leaving!"

"Aaron!" Mags called.

Her tone caught me by surprise. I turned, seeing pain in her eyes. In that moment I knew she believed completely in what she was about to say.

"Your Grandpa only wants what's best for you. I don't fully understand everything that's happening and I doubt you do either. But I do know that he cares about you and if he feels you'd be safer here, I think you should listen."

"Yeah." Raj interjected. "I don't want to see my best friend get messed up. If these people can protect you, maybe you should consider staying with them. Besides, it's not like you'd be going away forever. You can learn what they have to teach you and come back."

I felt betrayed by everyone. Grandpa had orchestrated all of this. My failed birthday party, my parents leaving. Heck, even the fact that I had magic was his fault. And now he was telling me I had to abandon my life to study at some place I knew nothing about, with people who couldn't possibly care anything about me. All they cared about was the magic in my blood, provided that was how it worked. I didn't actually know. And to make matters worse, Raj and Mags were okay with me leaving. No! I wasn't going to give up everything I knew just because some unknown threat wanted to use me for whatever end. I didn't know much but I knew living in fear was no way to live.

My fists clenched and my jaw tightened. I was about to give all of them a piece of my mind when a soft knock echoed from the door nearest the couch.

Grandpa calmly approached and twisted the knob. "What can we do for you, Alice?" He pulled the door open and allowed the white robed woman inside. I recognized her as the one who'd been speaking when we were in the chamber.

"I would have word privately, if that's okay?"

Grandpa glanced our way and signaled for us to turn around.

I wasn't sure what good it would do. The room wasn't very large and turning wouldn't do anything to keep us from hearing. We obliged anyway. To my surprise, I could barely hear more than a whisper when they began speaking.

With our backs turned and nothing else to do, I realized both Mags and Raj were focused on me. "What?" I finally asked, hoping they'd quit staring. All I wanted was to go home and forget any of this had ever happened.

"Are you okay?" Mags asked. I couldn't help but notice she'd been acting weird lately. Granted, the discovery of magic was inherently a weird thing to accept. She had every right to be a little off, but it seemed like it was more than that.

I did the only thing I knew to do. I shrugged. "I don't know. I'm not overly happy about you guys telling me to switch schools. I don't know these people and I definitely don't trust them. You should have heard one of the guys in there—" I gestured toward the warded and sealed door. "—he couldn't have cared if I got taken or not. He said I was making it all up. And then you guys team up against me and say I should listen to this ridiculous plan. No, thank you!"

"I'm not saying you should do everything your grandpa says, but I know he cares. I don't want anything bad to happen to you. I can tell he feels the same. That's the only reason I think you should listen." Mags had tears in her eyes. I wanted to hug her but I didn't want my intentions misconstrued.

"I think she's right." Raj added. "Besides, who would have thought all of this was real? You have to admit it's pretty awesome. Most people could only dream of such adventure and here we are smack in the middle. Like out of everyone, we're the ones who get to experience it."

I shook my head. "I just want to go home. Having adventures is all well and good when you can control what happens. When you can't—it's not as fun as I thought it would be."

"What do you mean, they declined the vote? I demand an appeal, immediately!" Grandpa shouted, which caught me off guard. I'd rarely heard him raise his voice and now he was full on yelling.

"Giles, I told you this as a courtesy. You have no right to raise your voice to me!" Alice retorted.

"I know. I apologize. Please, I need you to press the appeal. If they won't listen to reason I'll convince them with logic."

Alice sighed. "I'll table your appeal but I doubt it will do any good. Aleister is playing everything he can against you."

"Don't worry about him. Just get me in front of the grays. I'll handle the rest."

Alice nodded and turned toward the door. She paused at the threshold and glanced back. "Good luck, Giles."

"Aaron." Grandpa called, watching the door close. He turned to look upon me. "I understand your desire to remain with your friends but I need you to grasp the severity of your situation. You will never be safe until you learn to fully harness your abilities. It should be as second nature to you as breathing. A master wizard is able to think consciously even while sleeping. He can counter any spell cast at him while in his weakest state. Until you're able to do all of this and more, you'll spend the rest of your life looking over your shoulder. Waiting—dreading—anticipating the day when someone or something finds you. Do you want that?"

I thought about what he was saying. I was beginning to understand what he meant. It was a scary world I'd become a part of. I didn't like it one bit, but it seemed what I liked or wanted didn't matter anymore. "No, I don't want to live that way."

"Then I fear the only option is for you to work with me and convince them to give you the enrollment exam early. If they agree, you become off limits to anyone who might seek to harm you. Nobody would dare go against the council. To do so is to sign a death warrant."

"Is there any way to give up my powers? If I don't have them nobody can use me."

"If only it were that simple. Unfortunately, even if you were stripped, they'd just return in time. Magic is as much a part of you as the air you breathe or the water you drink. You cannot survive without it." Grandpa sighed, showing me a moment of defeat. In that moment my belief in him was stronger than any moment prior.

"I fear this is the only way. You must be granted sanctuary under enrollment. Anything else is a temporary solution. The strength of power you radiate will serve as a beacon, calling the forces of darkness like ships in a storm to a lighthouse."

My gaze broke and settled on the floor. I didn't like it one bit but what else could I do? "Fine. I'll take their stupid test. But as soon as I learn to control it, I'm gone."

I would have said more but at that moment a booming knock shook the walls and I watched the seal fall away from the inner door.

"The council has reached a verdict. Would the Wizard and Novice Corey return to garner response?"

Grandpa approached the open door and placed his hand on my shoulder as he had not long before. "Let's see this through."

We were guided inside, only this time Mags and Raj followed. No one said a word. We approached the central platform and waited for the council to begin.

One of the gray robed wizards stood and addressed us. "Giles Corey, Retired Wizard of the Third Order and Master of the White Arts, we have discussed your proposal in great detail. The council has come to a decision regarding the enrollment, and by extension, sanctuary of the novice, Aaron Corey. It is with deep regret that I must inform you, the novice is denied admittance until such a time as he has bound his arcanum and may properly undergo the enrollment examination. Understand, this decision was made by majority rule of the Council of Nine and does not reflect the opinions of any individual member of the council, nor the body over which we govern. I understand that you have been informed of this decision and have requested appeal. Be that correct?"

"It is."

"Very well. I open the floor to statements, recounts, and details you or your company believe may serve to alter this decision in any way."

"Thank you, Councilor Gavin.

"I would first like to thank you for your time in this regard. This is an extremely serious issue, one which I believe needs to be measured with the utmost clarity and careful consideration.

"It is true, my grandson has yet to bond to his arcanum. It is also true he was able to not only read its contents, but passively cast a spell from within by sheer happenstance without bonding. The strength required for such a feat is unheard of. I feel I need not mention the strength of power emanating from him even now. He's the strongest naturally born wizard in well over a century. It would be foolish to allow this council to overlook such merit. Why not train him? Why not ensure he safely arrives at his station, an asset to the wizarding world?"

"Yeah! What good is he going to be if something or someone slits his throat in the middle of the night?" Raj added unhelpfully.

Grandpa signaled him to be silent and for once I agreed.

"I know most of you personally. Some of us may not see eye to eye, but all of you know that I'm not one to exaggerate the severity of this situation. I humbly ask you reconsider this decision. See that this boy is of greater value as a free thinking wizard in league with this council, rather than some pawn in use simply to tip the scales of balance."

I watched the faces of the men and women silently judging me. Grandpa was getting through to them and while I didn't like the idea of having to leave everything I knew behind, however briefly, I now understood the importance of it. I only hoped he could sway them enough to change the vote.

"Novice Corey—Aaron, would you like to say anything?" Alice asked with a smile.

I thought for a long moment trying to find the words. There was so much to say, I didn't know where to begin. Moreover, how much was too much and what details were important to speak freely? Surely some needed to be reserved. I'd played chess with Grandpa long enough to know that just because you could make a certain move didn't mean you should. Oftentimes it was best to let your opponent make the first move so you could form a strategy to counteract them.

I found myself wondering if that was why he'd always challenged me. Was he teaching me to think strategically even before any of this had started?

After a long moment's silence, I found my voice. "Ladies and gentlemen of the jury—council—whatever. My name is Aaron Corey. Before today I was just a normal kid. I went to a normal school, and hung out with my normal friends. I did my homework most of the time. I played games and watched videos and did normal stuff normal people of my age do. I like being normal. I like being simple. It means I don't have to worry about much. And if today had gone as intended, I would still be normal.

"Today was my thirteenth birthday. For most kids my age that means pizza parties, games, and talking about a secret crush when that person isn't around." I glanced at Mags and turned away when our eyes met. "I had no idea about magic. I thought it was just some silly thing we used in our games to make them more entertaining. But now that I know it's real, I'd give anything to get rid of it. I don't want magic. I want to be a normal kid with a normal life and go to a normal school with other normal kids.

"I'm told that's not possible. I'm told even if I somehow found a way to get rid of my magic, it'd just come back. That leaves me in a mighty fine predicament. So, if the only way for me to move on with my normal life and get this crap under control is for me to go to your school, so be it. I'll do what I have to do. But if you think I'm going to lay back and let whatever's out there get me because of this power inside me, power that I don't even want, you're delusional. I don't care if you decide to accept me or not. I'll fight anybody that comes after me. I'll fight until I can't fight anymore. And if you don't like that you can kiss my butt!"

"That was a bit much, you think?" Raj leaned in to ask.

"No. They need to hear what's on my mind." I surveyed their faces to find mixed responses. It was about how I'd expected. The black robed wizards looked angry, like I'd insulted them. The whites were trying not to smile. And the grays appeared indifferent. Even Grandpa was smiling, though he hid it as quick as he could.

"Very well. Are there any other comments?" Gavin asked.

Mags raised her hand, timidly at first, then she fully committed to it.

"Yes, my dear?"

"I'd just like to say that Aaron is one of the most courageous people I know. He usually stands up for what he believes in and while he sometimes can be led astray, I'm happy to call him my friend. You guys would be lucky to have him here."

Our eyes met and she turned away, trying not to blush.

"Noted. Anyone else?"

Silence filled the room.

"Very well. At this time the council calls for a vote. By show of hands, using the official voting signal of the council, those in favor of appealing the initial vote and granting the novice wizard, Aaron Corey, the enrollment examination.

A few hands went up. I counted all three whites, and two grays, one of them being Gavin. If I was understanding the process correctly, it was five against four. That was majority which meant victory. It was for this reason I didn't understand when Gavin spoke again.

"Those opposed?"

A total of five hands were raised, all the blacks and two of the grays, including one who'd already voted.

"Eliphas, you voted for both." Gavin said, directing his attention to the gray wizard on the furthest left.

All eyes fell on the man. He sighed heavily, staring at the floor. Finally, he slowly raised his hand and spoke, refusing to meet anyone's gaze. "I vote against. Novice Corey is denied asylum."

"What?" Grandpa shouted.

The council chamber broke into a roar of chatter. It seemed everyone but me was yelling. I didn't know what to say. I didn't know what to feel. If this was the only way for me to remain safe, what chance did I have now? I was lost—numb. I didn't know what to do and everyone around me was busy in a shouting match.

"Silence!" A deafening voice boomed through the round shaped room, shaking the walls and floor. It didn't take a genius to realize it was magically altered.

The voices died down and once again the room fell quiet, save for grandpa who refused to obey.

"Clearly he's been tampered with. Why else would he vote for both and then change it last minute? I demand immediate replacement and a revote!"

"Wizard Corey, please. We'll get to the bottom of this." Gavin assured.

"There's nothing to get to the bottom of. We voted and the appeal failed. Why are you wasting our time with this nonsense?" Aleister interjected.

"I've heard enough. This council used to stand for order—used to stand for justice. Clearly it's fallen to corruption. I'll not stand idle and allow its ruin to spill over into the lives of the people I care about! Come, children." Grandpa started toward the door.

"Giles!" Aleister yelled. "Interference applies to both sides. Remember that before you step in and do something you'll regret."

Grandpa barely waited for the door to be opened before he shuffled out into the waiting room. As we passed through the doorway I found myself standing, not in the waiting room as expected, but back in Grandpa's tower with no idea how I'd gotten there.

# Chapter 10
## First Blood

It took a few moments before I realized where we were. I looked around the cool yet comfortable stone palace Grandpa called home. We were standing in the study once again just a few feet from the fireplace that crackled and sent an orange glow across the room.

"Um, Grandpa, if we could just teleport or whatever, why did we take the carriage in the first place?"

"Two reasons. First, they sent the carriage for us. It would have been rude to decline which wouldn't have helped our cause, not that it did any good anyway. And secondly, magical travel to the council chamber is strictly forbidden. Leaving on the other hand is less troublesome. Besides, after all that I doubt they would have provided transportation back."

"I guess that makes sense."

"What do we do now?" Mags asked, showing more concern than any of us.

"There isn't much we can do. Aleister made it clear that I'm not to interfere. It's a gray area. He wants me in this position. If I train Aaron some could claim I'm influencing his decisions. If I protect him, I'm doing the same. It leaves me with a difficult choice. I either have to abandon you three and hope that Aaron can figure things out on his own, or hold my ground and potentially face the council's wrath."

"What does their wrath look like?" I was fairly certain I already knew the answer but I couldn't help but ask. Either way, I knew things were about to get much more complicated.

"They would first issue an arrest order. Once I'm apprehended, they'd place me in a dampening collar to strip my power until a criminal trial can take place. Then, depending on the outcome of the trial, and having seen the council's corruption I take to be least favorable, I'd likely spend the remainder of my days funneling my magic into an arcane bank until I have nothing left to give, at which point I would eventually die."

"What are you going to do?" Raj joined the conversation. He was starting to understand the dire circumstances we were in and it showed.

"That's easy. Retired or not, I'm still a wizard of the third order and master of the white arts. I'll not be bullied into inaction by Aleister or any other. We have limited time before they infiltrate this place. I suggest we use it to the fullest."

"How's that?"

"We need to get you trained and bonded. I may not have the resources that the council does but I've acquired enough knowledge over the years to at least get you a decent start. Beyond that, it's up to you."

I knew this was one of those moments where everything was about to change. I could feel it in the air. I could see it in the numerous sparks that danced and fizzled around me. I could smell it—a strong musky scent, like a forest right after a heavy rain. Something big was about to happen. I just didn't know what. "Where do we begin?"

"I've found the best way to begin anything is with research. Knowledge is power. You've already touched on the history of magic. We certainly don't have time to go in-depth on anything, therefore, I think the best use of your time would be served in learning to identify the arcane schools. There are believed to be twelve in total, though you'll only find thorough information on eight of them within my library. Each school has its own characteristics. Once you can identify them individually, you'll have a better understanding as to their utilization. You'll find books on the subject right over there." Grandpa pointed to a series of bookshelves behind his lounge chair.

"What about us?" Raj asked, clearly wanting something to do.

"You two can help me build an obstacle course in the training room."

"Awesome!"

Raj and Mags followed Grandpa out of the study, leaving me to my solitude.

I have to admit it was a little overwhelming being left to my own devices. In a way their absence made it easier for me to focus. Up until now I'd been in the company of others. Even if they weren't talking, I still felt as if every move I made was being watched. That didn't help when it came to doing anything that could be potentially embarrassing. I just needed to remember not to read anything aloud. The last thing I wanted was to get teleported again.

I spent what felt like the next few hours reading little passages, learning everything I could about the various schools of magic. Some were enjoyable, others less so. I was surprised by how much knowledge crossed over from our game. The schools were named almost the same with minor differences, but each of them did about the same things. Between my joint knowledge from our game and what I'd found in Grandpa's books, I'd used magics, intentional or not, from the Abjuration, Conjuration, Divination, and Evocation schools. And since I knew how to identify them, I now knew which energies to pull when I wanted to use them.

I still didn't understand the other schools Grandpa had mentioned. There wasn't much I could find about them. I knew one of them had to be necromancy. Its use was frowned upon in most game settings. It stood to reason the same would apply in the real world. Most people weren't keen on the idea of raising the dead or using negative energies to harm others.

The other missing schools were even more evasive. I'd found a minor reference about *the lost art of time* and another involving the use of blood to fuel spells but even if those were missing schools, I couldn't fathom what the others were.

I was getting tired of reading. I'm pretty sure I was getting tired in general. I had no idea what time it was in the outside world but I felt like I'd been awake for weeks and all this studying wasn't helping anything.

I set the book aside and my gaze settled on a ceramic mug that had been resting on the end table beside Grandpa's chair since before our arrival. I found myself wishing it was one of the goblets that would fill itself with little more than a thought. I was desperate for some hot chocolate with tons of marshmallows.

An idea came to me. Gritting my teeth, I pulled at the little orange specks lingering around the empty mug. Slowly, I forced them into the material. They began to take shape and the mug started to shake. As the final sparks fell into place, they flashed and disappeared. What had been a white mug with brownish markings was now transparent glass.

"Dammit!" Irritated by my failure, I swatted the mug off the table. To my surprise, it never crashed to the floor. Instead, I turned to find it floating back toward the table.

"You cannot allow yourself to become discouraged. It will not help your focus." Grandpa was standing at the entrance behind me, his hand contorted and guiding the mug back where it belonged. "That was a fine transmutation you performed. Though judging by your outburst, I take it you were attempting something different?"

"I wanted to fill it with hot chocolate."

"I see. Well, transmutation is not the school for such a thing. It's used for turning one thing into another. Had the mug a liquid in it, such a thing would have been possible. You should have attempted a conjuration, calling your desire from a different location. Try it again, only this time focus on the blue sparks instead of the orange."

I'd had about all the *trying* I could stand for one evening. With a sigh, I decided to give it a final shot.

Focusing on the energies around the now transparent glass, I isolated the blue flecks and pulled them into the void within the cup. I focused intently on filling it with hot chocolate and marshmallows. To my surprise a brownish liquid with white blobs began to fill the mug. I kept pulling until it was near the brim. When it reached the top, I released the blue specks and felt the spell disperse, leaving my drink behind. In excitement I grabbed the altered mug and tipped it to my lips.

"Very good. But can you do that while someone is trying to kill you?" Grandpa asked with a satisfied smirk on his face.

"Just let me have this one!" I snapped unintentionally. I didn't know if it was because I'd been up all night, because I'd been doing so much reading, or if it was because the spellwork was exhausting me. If it was anything like my game there was only so much casting I could do before I'd simply be out.

"Sorry." I said, realizing I'd bitten a little too hard over something so trivial. "I'm just tired. Where's Mags and Raj?"

"They fell asleep in the training room about thirty minutes ago. I thought it best to let them sleep. There isn't much they can do right now anyway. As for being tired, it's understandable but I'm afraid you can't sleep until you've learned to protect yourself while consciously unavailable." Grandpa started walking toward me with a coffee mug that looked eerily like the one I'd turned transparent, though this one still had its ceramic colors.

"How am I supposed to do that?"

"Have you ever heard of lucid dreaming?"

"What, like controlling my dreams?"

"Yes, but it's so much more than that. It's called Oneiromancy. By learning how to lucid dream you can take control of your dreams while asleep, control of your physical body while in a dream state, or even bring the dream into waking life. While in dreamstate your consciousness exist more like an astral projection where you exist in multiple places at the same time. From this state you can protect yourself while allowing your body to recharge."

"How am I supposed to learn this if I'm not allowed to sleep?"

"You can't. Lucid dreaming is a practiced skill, one which can take months, or even years to master."

"So what, I'm not going to be able to sleep ever again?"

"No." Grandpa extended the mug. "I'm going to help you. Drink this."

I eyed the murky concoction suspiciously. It had some loose leaves floating in it and it smelled like tea. "What's in it?"

"Just a few herbs that will put you into a lucid state."

I wasn't sure how this was going to help. If I wasn't allowed to sleep because I couldn't protect myself, why was he giving me something to put me to sleep?

My mind began to wander and I couldn't help but think this was some kind of test. Or worse, what if one of my enemies had somehow infiltrated the tower? "How do I know you're you and this isn't some kind of trick to get me to let my guard down?"

Grandpa smiled. "I'm glad to see you're starting to think strategically. I'm proud that you're suspicious of such. To prove my validity, when you beat me in chess earlier today, your queen trapped my king in what's called a Fool's Mate on position H4. It was the first time you've ever beaten me."

I didn't know much about illusion magic but I suspected there was no way to mimic memories in such detail without great effort, and since Grandpa wasn't currently channeling some divination spell, I believed it was really him. "Okay." I set my hot chocolate down and took the mug he was holding. Bringing it to my lips, I tipped it back.

Before I could question anything, I found myself standing at the edge of a lake, looking out over the water. Trees swayed in the distance and an inverted rainbow pointed to a pot of gold at the center of a small island.

A part of me wanted to go to the island but I knew the leprechaun would chase me if I went near it. Instead, I simply watched from where I stood, waiting for the behemoth creature in green to lose interest and go back to sleep.

"Aaron." A familiar voice called from somewhere far away. It drifted in and out on the breeze and I didn't bother to look for it.

"Aaron." The voice repeated, much closer this time. I turned to the right where my grandpa was standing, staring at me. He looked younger and wore a funny expression on his face. I wondered if he'd always looked like that or if it was a new development.

The world around me changed in an instant and I found myself standing in the visitor's lounge of his retirement home. The chess board was set with a Fool's Mate on the board and all three of the TVs were displaying a static image with no sound.

"Aaron, you're dreaming." Grandpa said. He was sitting at the table and I found myself sitting across from him as I always did.

"Listen to me, lad. Remember what I told you. You're dreaming. Take control of the dream."

"What?" He wasn't making any sense.

"You're dreaming. You need to take control."

"That's silly. I'm not dreaming. I'm wide awake. See?" I pinched myself but to my surprise it didn't hurt. Actually, I couldn't feel it at all. "Weird."

"Listen to me. You need to take control of the dream. You have to protect yourself."

Flashes of memory filled my mind. I remembered the dark forest and the council. I remembered the shield spell that I'd used to counter my own energy bolt. Faster than conscious thought, pieces came together. I shot from my chair with sudden and immediate purpose. "I'm dreaming!"

"Yes. Now, don't wake up yet. I need you to open yourself to the world around you."

I closed my eyes, trying to focus. The world of detail drifted away. I was in the dream world. Everything was hazy, like I was staring through a fog bank, or at the center of a cloud looking out.

"That's it. You're almost there. Keep going."

I strained, trying to find myself. Somewhere in the haze I spotted a thin green thread. It had a glossy reflectivity to it.

"Yes! That's what you're looking for. It's your life line. Be careful with it. Anytime you find yourself lost in an astral state simply find that line and follow it back to your body. But make sure you protect it. If it ever gets cut you won't be able to find your way back."

I gently pulled on the line, guiding myself through the fog like a boat coming to shore. After a few short moments I saw myself, lying unconscious in the chair I'd been sitting. My head was drooped to the side and I had a mild amount of drool running down my cheek.

"Good. Now, create a shield like you did earlier. Lock it around your body so that no one can harm you while you're asleep."

I found the white energies and began pulling them together into a sort of cocoon that wrapped around my body. No sooner than the last piece settled in, the entire thing glowed brightly and held fast. I knew I'd done it. I'd managed to shield myself while unconscious.

"Good. Now wake up."

I opened my eyes feeling completely refreshed. I have no idea how long I was out but it felt like a full night in the comfort of my bed. My shield remained locked in place.

Memories of the dream rushed to the front of my mind, every detail falling into place like conscious memory. I looked around to find Grandpa standing where I last remembered him. "How do I do that without someone telling me I'm dreaming?"

"It takes time, but the easiest way is to do exactly what you did that time. Create a tell that you use every time you're unsure. You pinched yourself which triggered the realization. If that works for you, great. Some people use a spinning top. If it falls over, they're awake. Some people spin a coin. It doesn't matter what it is, you just have to find something that's unique to you. If you use it every time you suspect you're asleep, it'll tell you the truth."

A loud crash echoed from somewhere in the distance and the tower shook so hard I nearly fell out of my chair. Catching myself, I stared up at Grandpa who looked just as concerned as I was. "What was that?"

"They're here."

"Who?"

"Those who want you. It could be the council. It could be anyone."

"I thought you said this place was safe."

"It was for a time. No place can hold indefinitely. Go, wake your friends if they're not up already. I have a few counter measures to prepare for when they get through."

I jumped to my feet and broke into a sprint. I immediately wished I'd paid a little closer attention the last time I'd passed through these halls. They all looked the same. I turned left, then right, then left again. I passed large rooms, small rooms, rooms inside other rooms, each filled with a wide assortment of knickknacks and gadgets to which I couldn't even guess the function. After what I suspected was numerous wrong turns I found myself in a familiar room. I was back in the study.

"Um, Grandpa, which way is the training room?"

He looked up from some large paper that was trying to roll up on him. "Take the third left and go down the stairs. From there, it doesn't matter which door you go through, they'll all take you to the training rooms."

I turned and started down the hall a second time when another blast knocked me off my feet. I slammed into the wall and dropped to the floor. Fortunately, my shield took the brunt of the damage and I didn't feel anything more than a mild pressure.

Picking myself up, I continued on, following the directions Grandpa had given me. Sure enough, at the bottom of the stairs I found a series of doors, all leading to my destination.

Mags was standing near one of the small port windows trying to look outside when I arrived. "Aaron, what's happening?"

"Someone's trying to get in. Grandpa told me to come get you guys. Where's Raj?"

"I don't know. He was gone by the time I awoke."

"Okay. Hold still. That last blast was pretty hard. I'm going to put a shield around you in case it knocks you off your feet." I placed my hands on Mags' arms and began to focus. It was coming much easier this time and the pieces fell into place almost on their own. I watched the shield solidify, and checked to make sure my own was still active at the same time. Content in our protection, regardless of how minor it was, I took her by the hand and started for one of the numerous entryways. We had to find Raj before he got himself into trouble.

We passed through hallways and rooms, corridors and ramps, balconies and stairs. He was nowhere to be found.

"Raj!" I yelled, hoping he'd answer. There was no reply. With a heavy sigh, I stopped and turned to face Mags. "I don't know where he is and we can't spend the rest of the night looking for him. I was reading up on the various types of magic. Do you think it's possible for us to summon him?"

"Aaron, that's a big risk I wouldn't feel comfortable taking. What if we make a mistake? You know the rules. We don't know where he is or where he'd appear. What if we put him halfway inside a wall or something like that? Or worse, what if we summoned the wrong him. Like an older or younger version, or maybe a Raj from an alternate dimension if such a thing exist. There are too many unknown variables and you don't have enough experience to try it."

I nodded agreement. I was glad to have her here. She was always the most logical among us and I knew I wouldn't have made it this far without her. "You're right. I'm sorry. I need to start thinking of things like that first."

"It's okay. This is new to all of us. It's going to take some time getting used to." She smiled and squeezed my arm.

The tower shook a third time and I heard stone crumble. Considering the walls and floor didn't shake like they had before I knew the tower had been breached. That meant the enemy was inside.

"We need to get back to Grandpa now. Hopefully we'll find Raj on the way."

Mags and I followed the path we'd taken back to the training room. Just as I was about to enter the stairwell, Grandpa appeared in front of me.

"There you are. We need to get out of here. The tower's defenses have been defeated. Where's your friend? The dark haired one?"

"We don't know. He wasn't here when I arrived."

"Damn that boy!" That was the first time I'd heard Grandpa cuss. He let out an exhausted sigh before perking up with a new idea. "We'll find him. Until then we need to buy some time. Hurry to the other side of the obstacle course."

We moved along the left side of the training room to one of the wings where a flying swarm of energy balls darted around us.

How nothing hit us, I didn't know but I felt a few close calls. I just hoped my shield was strong enough to protect us.

We hunkered down behind what looked to be a large padded dummy. Grandpa turned to us.

"No matter what happens or what you hear, stay right here. I'll be back in a moment." And with that, he was gone.

I lay against the dummy, half holding Mags, half worried about what was going to happen next. I'd learned a little, sure. But was it enough to fend off whatever had the power to blast its way into the tower?

Before I could spend a second longer on the thought, a booming voice tore through the air and I had to shield my ears to block it out. Even then it helped minimally.

"Attention all occupants, be they intruder or guest. The tower has fallen. Surrender yourselves now by placing your hands above your head and reciting the words, 'I submit.' Any occupant who fails to adhere to this simple task will be met with deadly force!"

I recognized Grandpa's voice though it was amplified greatly. A part of me wanted to do what the message suggested. I suspected it was some kind of compulsion spell, though I hadn't learned enough about them to know for certain.

Mags started to raise her hands and I had to fight to pin them down. "I have to, Aaron. It's a simple task that will be met with deadly force if ignored!" She demanded, struggling to get free.

That solidified my theory. There was no way she would have spoken those words so closely if it hadn't been part of a spell. Still. I had to keep her from doing it. I didn't know what would happen but I didn't want her to find out, especially after Grandpa told us to stay here.

Unfortunately she was so strong, I was having trouble overpowering her. That left one option. I had to break the compulsion by other means. I leaned in and pressed my lips to hers. She struggled for a moment and then gave in. We held each other for the briefest moment—a moment that felt like eternity. And when I pulled away she didn't fight me any longer.

"What was that?" She asked as if suddenly awakened from sleep.

"I—um—you—you were under a spell. I had to do that to break it."

"Sure." She said with emphasis, trailing off with a smile. "I bet you just wanted to kiss me."

"Nuh uh." I blushed and turned away so she wouldn't see.

Grandpa appeared in the place he'd been a moment before, only now he had Raj with him.

"Where have you been?" Mags snapped.

"I went exploring. I found a room full of telescopes and a bunch of crystals. It was cool."

Without hesitation, Mags reached out and punched him in the arm.

"Ouch. Stop doing that!"

"I will when you stop doing stupid stuff. In case you haven't noticed, we're in danger. We could have been better prepared for it by now if we didn't have to stop everything and waste time finding you."

"I'm sorry, okay. I just wanted to see what else this place had."

I felt kind of bad for Raj. He was always the one to wander off, and it usually got him in trouble. Why was now any different? On the other hand I could see Mags' point as well. We didn't know what was coming and those precious moments we spent looking for him could have been used elsewhere.

"I'm here now. What's the plan?"

"We didn't have enough time for Aaron to learn everything I wanted to teach him. And considering these attackers were able to overcome my defenses, I take it they were also smart enough to place antitravel sigils before they ever started. That eliminates most traveling spells. There are a few that could still get us through but they take some time to cast." Grandpa materialized a rolled scroll from out of nowhere and gestured with it as if it were the solution to our problem.

"That's why I brought us here. This obstacle course was designed to test Aaron in every way. A master magician won't have near as much trouble with it, but it will still take effort and time to navigate. If we're to make it out, I'm going to need all three of you to help me cast this spell." Grandpa started unrolling the scroll.

The parchment was thick and brown from age. It looked like the slightest movement might make it crumble to dust, and the ink that had soaked into the fibers glowed an almost blue hue that brought renewed strength to the otherwise worn page. When it was fully stretched out it was nearly as tall as Grandpa and about a quarter as wide.

I had no idea how we were supposed to read it. Even if Raj and Mags knew what it said, they weren't magical. What was their participation supposed to do?

As if Grandpa had read my thoughts, he began to explain. "You may be wondering why I need all three of you. The simple answer is all of us need to escape. Therefore, we all need to read it. The more complex answer is, it's a matter of numbers. An antitravel sigil is no different than any other spell. It can be overpowered by a more powerful spell. A single caster is unlikely to possess enough power to do this, but two casters in cooperation with two assistants can easily overpower such a sigil."

"Giles Corey, I know you're in there. Surrender yourselves and I guarantee most of you will survive." I knew that voice. It had been the last voice I heard before we left the council chamber.

"Aleister." Grandpa said with distain. "I knew he had to be involved. He's the only dark wizard on the council with the power to pull off something like this."

A bolt of red energy flew across the room and exploded on the stone wall behind us. I thought it strange considering most evocation spells imploded, but a few, specifically of the fire variety had a tendency to explode.

Another whizzed past and I felt the heat of it.

"What are we gonna do? I don't think we have enough time to read this." Mags asked, ducking as another firebolt flew past.

"We fight. They still have to get through the course before they can reach us. We may as well make it harder on them." I prepared myself, taking a mental note of the obstacles and places to seek cover. It wasn't much of a plan but it was better than waiting to be barbequed.

Grandpa started to object but a firebolt interrupted him. It tore through the scroll and the ancient paper disintegrated in his hands. With our only escape now lost to us, fighting was the only remaining option.

"What about us?" Mags asked, looking helpless. It was a look that didn't become her. She was never helpless and I didn't much like seeing her that way. I closed my eyes and envisioned my desire. I don't know how I did it, or even how I knew what to grab. I just knew what belonged to her. Mags had claimed it earlier in the night. I was simply retrieving it for her.

Blue hues of energy began to materialize and in no time a golden suit of perfectly contoured armor was fixed around her. She had a warhammer in one hand and a medium sized shield in the other. More feeling than anything, I knew it was all magical and would protect her.

"Wow!" She smiled and I felt a sudden relief. She was as safe as I could make her and that made me happy.

"What about Raj?" Mags asked, turning her attention to him.

"Don't worry. I've got it covered." Raj reached into one of his many pockets and retrieved a familiar pair of gloves he'd found earlier. Slipping his hands inside, he smiled victory and took position behind one of the wooden devices on this end of the course.

"I thought I told you to put those back." Grandpa scowled, though it quickly turned to a smile. "I suppose it's a good thing you didn't listen. Just be careful with them. You've discovered one function but they do so much more than you realize."

"Like what?"

The lights dimmed and several spells flew overhead like a prismatic meteor shower, telling me there were multiple enemies on the other side of the room. I just hoped we could hold out until either they gave up or we found an alternative way out. I didn't know which was more likely, though neither had good odds.

"We don't have time to get into that now, but I'll show you everything they can do if we survive this." Grandpa assured with a serious tone. "The best option here is an all-out assault. If we all attack at the same time we'll stand a pretty good chance of taking down at least one. But don't linger. Fire your shot and get to cover."

I nodded my understanding but I was struggling with the butterflies in my stomach. This was the first real fight I'd been in and it seemed also the most serious. One wrong move and it could end in a flash. I wondered if the others felt the same.

I looked to Mags who was hunkered down beside me. She was confident in her shining armor and weapons of war. It inspired confidence in me.

Raj was just as ready with a wide smile on his face. He looked as if he'd been waiting his whole life for this exact moment.

I had no idea what Grandpa's initial plan was but seeing my friend so ready gave me an idea. There were numerous plans I'd either used or thought about using during our game and I was desperate to give them a try. I focused on my target and began collecting the energies required to make it happen. I just hoped it would work as I envisioned.

"Three—two—one!" Grandpa popped from his shelter and launched a series of rapid burst bolts from his fingers. They shot through a cloud of what looked to be black smoke and a figure at its center collapsed.

Mags spun around and pointed her hammer toward our attackers. I don't know how or why it happened, whether it was luck, or if Grandpa had had something to do with it, but a beam of light fired from the end and cut through the darkness. Unfortunately, it didn't appear to hit anyone but I was impressed nonetheless. It certainly sent a few of them running which was just as good in my opinion.

Raj struck a small red lighter and a short fuse began to burn away. He threw the firecracker over the obstacle course and almost immediately reached out with his gloved hand. The tiny explosive slowed and drifted between the waist band and flesh of one of the guys. He started dancing around and let out a howl as it exploded in his pants.

Taking a deep breath, I released the energies I'd been gathering. I watched a blue ring form on the floor under Aleister. It solidified and flashed and suddenly he fell through. A moment later, an identical ring appeared on the ceiling and he fell out only to fall into the first ring again.

I didn't know how long I could hold the portal open but I hoped it was long enough to deal with the rest of these guys. I didn't particularly want to kill him, which I had some fear over. If the discussions on the tactic were correct, he'd gain speed each time he passed through. After five or six passes he'd reach terminal velocity and either suffocate from inability to breathe or he'd splat on the ground when the spell ended.

A part of me wished I'd thought about that before I'd placed him in such a position. Then again, he'd already threatened death upon us. Was it really so wrong if my actions resulted in his demise? I wasn't sure and I hoped I wouldn't have the opportunity to find out. I just needed him out of the way for as long as possible.

# Chapter 11
## Cost of Admission

The floor in this part of Grandpa's tower looked to be more of the same gray stone I'd seen in other parts of the expansive fortress. It was worn flat with time and the grout lines were thin and nearly impossible to see. Were it not for the collected dust changing their color I had no doubt they would have been all but invisible.

I was wedged in a corner between one of the stone walls, more defined than the floor beneath, and a collection of wooden barrels that provided some measure of protection. The training dummies weren't far, shielding Mags and Grandpa. Raj had taken position behind a stack of barrels against the other wall.

Bolts of red, blue, green, and just about every other color of energy flew overhead. I had no doubt one tiny miscalculation, or popping up at the wrong moment would be all it took to end my existence.

I glanced at Raj, then at Mags. They were pinned down just the same and I desperately hoped neither would be so foolish as to risk it. We'd made a decent dent in our initial assault, but it wasn't enough. There were more of them than any of us could have expected.

Some looked like ordinary people, dressed in what I would have considered normal clothes. Others clung to the old style and were dressed in robes of black or gray, though far more of the former. A few were strange looking creatures that I could only guess at. There were vicious looking beasts, some covered in thick mangy fur, while others had wispy thin coats that revealed spotted, speckled, and sometimes scarred skin beneath.

Probably the most terrifying of all was the shadow creatures. They were a thick dark smoke that looked vaguely humanoid shaped and had sharp talons of ivory that appeared and disappeared faster than the eye could see. Thus far I'd only seen one of them go down and what was left was a jelly looking mass that hissed and bubbled as it disappeared between the minute cracks of the stone floor.

We'd woefully underestimated our opponents and now we were paying for it.

The only wild card was Grandpa. He hadn't given so much as a thought since our first attack and he hadn't really done much other than throw shields over us anytime an untimely blast came a little too close for comfort. If he were to ever fully unleash, I wondered what he'd be capable of.

And of course, there was Aleister, still trapped in my pitfall, though I didn't know for how long and I was somewhat afraid to let him out.

"Grandpa—" I shouted. "We can't stay here. There's too many of them."

"I'm working on that, just keep your heads down!"

I counted down in my head, timing their shots. I still had my shield up. I knew it was a risk but if it couldn't absorb at least one blow, what good was it?

I lunged out and fired off a quick lightning bolt. It struck one of the black robed wizards in the chest and sent him flying back. The arcs shot to two others but it didn't appear to do much more than daze them. That was enough. I just needed the distraction.

I rushed from my cover, forming a disc shield over my already fractured wrap and deflected two blasts that would have hit me center mass. Dropping to my knees, I slid into a better spot between two of the targeting dummies.

I hadn't noticed it originally but every now and then the dummies fired a random spell toward our attackers. I guessed those spells had been intended for me, which meant they probably weren't lethal, but something was better than nothing.

I moved to the edge of my cover and ducked low, peeking under one of the makeshift legs. I could see four guys within view, and who knew how many beyond that.

"Aaron, brace yourself." Grandpa yelled over the constant barrage of spellfire.

I felt the air around me shift. It began to get warm and tighten, and then I saw the blue sparks and I realized what was happening. Grandpa had somehow found a way to transport us out of here.

I crashed into the cold floor of a dark room that still felt remarkably like stone.

"Um, Grandpa?"

"Yes?"

"Are we still in the tower?"

"Yes. The antitravel sigils have us locked within these walls but that doesn't mean we can't move within its confines."

About that time light flared up and my vision went white for the briefest moment. When it balanced out and my vision returned I saw a glowing orb floating over Grandpa's head.

"Where are we?" Raj asked, looking around at the multitude of barrels, crates, and shelves filling the dank room.

"My storeroom. I apologize we don't have nearly as much space in here but almost any component we might need is readily available. That may prove useful once they find us again."

"How are they going to do that?" I asked, fearing I already knew the answer.

"The same way they found us last time. They followed your power. And they'll continue to do so until you learn to properly shield yourself."

"I thought I already learned that part? I've been doing great in that department. They're getting to the point that I'm not really even having to try anymore."

"That's good, but you still have a long way to go. Shielding yourself means more than simply creating a barrier to stop damage. It means blocking all trace of your existence to anything you don't want to find you. You need to master yourself. Everything you do should be a reflex. Only then will those who know about you back off. And those who don't won't be able to read you."

"Um, guys—" Mags trailed off, pointing to a rather mysterious ring forming on the wall beside us.

"What's that?" Raj asked, reaching out to touch it.

"Don't!" Grandpa near yelled. "They've already found us. As soon as the circle finishes forming they'll be here and I don't have time to ready another teleport."

"What can we do?" I asked, looking for any defense or method to slow them down.

"Put as much stuff in the way as possible. I don't care what it is. Block the entrance. As soon as it opens, push as much through as you can. With any luck a few of them will get spliced."

"What's that mean?"

"It's where the magics of the dimensional tunnel fuse you with anything in the way." Grandpa clarified.

"So, so like a dim door into a wall. Got it." Raj smiled approvingly and took position to the side of the nearly complete circle. Tilting one of the filled barrels, he rolled the bottom edge right in front of the wall and started to grab another.

A zap echoed the moment the portal finished and a heap of bloody meat, bone, and barrel fragments spattered on the floor.

"That's disgusting!" Raj demanded, though the smile never left his face.

Mags buried her face in my shoulder. Instinctively I wrapped my arm around her. It was nice though I wish it would have happened under better circumstances. We'd just inadvertently killed someone and I didn't know how I was going to live with that.

Grandpa clapped his hands together and began contorting his fingers in an intricate weave. I wasn't sure what he was doing since none of the spells I'd worked thus far required such silly rituals. It was more or less just thought and focus, making the various energies obey my command. I wondered what doing such strange movements would do for my casting. Would it make them more powerful? Or was it simply something more powerful spells required?

Of course, I could have asked the same thing about verbal spells. I'd only used one so far and that was when I ended up at the forest's edge. Even then I didn't know if it was the verbal command or the accidental discharge that made it happen. I didn't remember pulling any of the colored sparks, but then again I couldn't see them prior to that.

Forcing the thoughts from my head, I watched several of the barrels explode into pieces of curved planks, metal rings, and a wide assortment of whatever contents had been in them. They lifted into the air with Grandpa's gesture and began to fire into and around the portal like a roman candle that refused to run out of shot.

"Go for the door!" Grandpa strained, sweat beading on his forehead. I could see he was getting visibly weaker and I suspected this was what happened when someone was running out of power. If that was the case, I feared what would come next.

Raj reached the wooden door and lifted the latch keeping it shut. He pulled the barricade toward him and stepped into the hall.

Mags was right on his tail, her glimmering armor reflecting the torchlight outside the tiny room.

"Aaron, go! I can't hold it much longer."

I didn't want to leave him. For all I knew they'd kill him on sight and I wasn't ready to lose my grandpa just yet. He had so much more to teach me. But he'd told me to go. I didn't know if I could obey that command. "What about you?"

"Don't worry about me. I'll be fine. It's you they're after."

I didn't like it but I ran.

It took only a few seconds to catch up with my friends. We followed the winding corridors, straying away from the clatter of boots and random booms that continued to echo throughout the tower. It sounded as if enemies were everywhere, still fighting, though I didn't know what. I was under the impression that the tower's defenses were already down so who were they fighting with?

We rounded a corner and found ourselves back in the study. I didn't know if that was a wise choice or not. Sure, it had a lot of books, but we didn't have time to read them. More importantly, it seemed every time I got turned around, I always seemed to find myself in the study, as if it was the center of the tower and all roads led to it. If that was the case, it seemed the bad guys could just as easily do the same.

Still, Mags seemed to regain some of her confidence in the firelit chamber of open balconies and walls of books.

That gave me an idea. "Guys, we need to go up there." I pointed to the balcony. "It's a perfect ambush position. We can blast anyone who comes through any of the doors. More importantly, when we were up there earlier, I didn't see any connecting doors which means they'll have a harder time sneaking up behind us."

"What if they open another one of those portal things?" Raj asked, unsure if any plan was going to be good enough.

"I don't think they will. That last one was probably a tracer spell. They could only use it because that's how we escaped. Had we not used magic, I don't think they would have been able to follow us so easily. Not with magic anyway." It was entirely a guess but it seemed reasonable enough to me. And it placated Raj, which was all I really needed at the moment. The loss of Grandpa had shaken all of us and we needed to remain calm if we were going to make it through this.

I started for the central stairs that led to the right side balcony. To my pleasure and relief, both Mags and Raj came with me. I wasn't sure they were going to. At the same time I suspected all any of us really wanted was for someone to take charge and give commands. That was all I wanted anyway. But nobody else had done it so I had to.

No sooner than we reached the top, I spun and started weaving the energies required to form a shield over the main doors, as well as the stairway we'd just marched. I wasn't sure if it would keep people out. It seemed to prevent damage of all kinds but I didn't know if it would do anything against someone simply walking through. Afterall, physical contact didn't seem to be affected but I had personal experience that it protected me from a fall. That made it worth trying at the very least. And if it didn't work I'd know better next time, provided I got a next time.

We huddled next to the wall right above the entrance doors. That seemed to make the most sense. We would be protected from sight until someone reached near center of the room. And anyone coming through the doors would be pelted from the moment they appeared until long after they reached the stairs. If they made it that far, there was a fairly long trek from the stairs to where we positioned.

Raj went to work grabbing the largest books he could find.

"What are you gonna do with those?" I asked, though the question answered itself the moment I'd vocalized it.

"I'm going to throw them at anyone who comes through that door."

"I see."

Mags stayed close to the wall, silently forming a plan. All she had was her warhammer and shield. Without Grandpa here to make it happen, I didn't expect her to get lucky with another light blast. Still, if she could hit any of our attackers, that was sure to slow them.

I waited in anticipation, unsure how much magic I had left in me. I was still new to this and I'd never run out before. I was exhausted, but I felt like I could still sling a few spells. Though I wasn't sure if it'd be just one or a hundred and one. With nowhere to go all I could do was fight until I couldn't fight anymore.

I heard footsteps in the hallway just outside the study and I prepared myself as best I could.

A blast of energy slammed into my hastily built shield and I watched it fracture. Another blast sent it scattering into pieces of glass-like energy that evaporated before it hit the floor.

Three men and one of the shadow beasts came walking through the door. We opened fire.

Raj began pelting them with books and firecrackers and stink bombs.

I flung the least taxing spells I could think of, simple plasma bolts that rained down over the entrance like a hailstorm. It appeared useful at the beginning but after the first few landed the wizards threw disc shields up and the bolts crashed harmlessly into them.

The books fared little better but the miniature explosives and stink bombs seemed to be having a much greater effect.

Raj crouched down and began working his gloved fingers like he was tying a knot.

Out of nowhere one of the normal clothed wizards tripped and fell. I heard his chin slam to the floor and he didn't get back up.

Searching for anyway to be effective, Mags closed her eyes and began whispering to herself. It took me a moment to realize she was praying which caught me off guard as I'd never known her to be the religious type, but I can't deny that it inspired a renewed burst of energy.

I suddenly felt as if I'd slept again. All the fatigue I'd suffered had faded away and I felt like I could blast these guys to oblivion if only I knew how.

She opened her eyes and for the briefest moment I could have sworn I saw a golden flash. Mags smiled at me and she raised the warhammer overhead. A pillar of golden light shot from it and exploded atop the shadow creature. It hissed in pain and burned away to a pile of ash that drifted harmlessly through the air.

"Wha—how—how'd you do that? Did you know you could do that?" I was shocked.

She chuckled. "No clue. I prayed for help and it just popped into my head. I figured I'd give it a shot and somehow it worked. Must be a magic hammer or something."

"Must be." I agreed, surveying our remaining foes. There were two of them left and to my displeasure one of them was Aleister. I couldn't help but wonder how he'd escaped my trap. I thought for certain I'd killed him. Then again, he was a master wizard and I barely knew how to make a shield.

It was time for me to do something cool. So far both Raj and Mags had done something useful and here I was, the one with magic and I hadn't even slowed them down.

The first guy was nearing the stairs when I got an idea. "Hang on to something!"

Drawing on the blue energies, I gathered as many as I could and created a swirling vortex. It took little more than a thought and they began to spin on their own. More and more joined the fray and a moment later a spinning tornado began to tear through the study, sucking up books and furniture, and thankfully the guy nearest the stairs right as he was attacking my barrier. I didn't know where it was spitting them out but it wasn't here. That was all I cared about. Unfortunately a green glowing field around Aleister kept him from being sucked away. He walked right through it as if it were nothing.

Books went scattering, drawn into the vortex. I could tell Raj and Mags were both shouting at me but I couldn't hear what they were saying. The roar of the wind was too loud.

Entire shelves were sucked up and disappeared in an instant and still Aleister kept walking toward us. He waved his hand and dismissed my pathetic excuse for a wall like it was nothing. Up the stairs he went, casually approaching without a care in the world.

Raj strained to keep his grip on the railing but even that was pulling free under such force.

Mags reached for him but it was too late. The entire section broke free and Raj disappeared into the swirling mass.

It happened so fast. I didn't have time to do anything but watch him plead for help.

Mags spun and grabbed hold of me, burying her face in my chest. I held her tight, knowing the pain she was feeling.

Something hit me. I stumbled back, catching myself against the wall. I could feel a trickle of blood running down my forehead but before I could do anything about it a book fell to the floor in front of me. I recognized the cover. It was the book Grandpa had given me. Of all the books in the study what was the chanced this particular one would hit me?

Careful to keep hold of Mags, I bent at the knees and retrieved it. Aleister was less than ten feet away from us now and I could see a victorious smirk on his face.

I stared at the book, unsure why it had come to me, then a dark red dot splattered on the cover. I had just a moment to see it before it soaked into the binding.

As if it had a mind of its own, it flew open to the entry page, the one Grandpa had asked me to read what felt so long ago. This time, rather than strange and unfamiliar symbols, normal English writing that was strangely similar to my handwriting appeared in its stead. With no other options, I read what it said.

*Whosoever binds this book shall Walk the Night, Calm the Night, and Control the Night, but not be Of the Night. For a wizard of this stature is among the rarest stock. He shall claim dominion of will and the soulless will march upon his command. For his home is death so long as he lives.*

I had no idea what any of it meant but I felt a strange sensation come over me. Before I could do anything about it a warm robe appeared in place of my clothes.

To my surprise Aleister came to a halt, a curious expression on his face. His head cocked to the side and he suddenly looked unsure of himself.

Tendrils of dark energy exploded from the floor all around him. They reached out and wrapped around his arms and legs, pulling him in all directions. They squeezed tight, pulsing as he screamed in despair. I could see a green energy being sucked from his withering body. A final cry escaped him and the tendrils released, disappearing back into the floor. He staggered, his now sticklike legs unable to hold his shriveled form.

I watched him collapse, his body turning to dust only to be wisped away by the vortex.

My eyes rolled into the back of my head and I felt my knees grow weak. I started to fall but Mags caught me as I blacked out.

The Wizard's Grandson

Levi Samuel

# Chapter 12
## Witch, Please

I was standing at the edge of a vast lake. A magnificent rainbow arched across the sky, ending at a giant pot of gold at the center of an island. An equally giant leprechaun kept pacing the perimeter.

I froze. This all seemed eerily familiar to me. Words whispered at the edge of my cognitive thought, though they were too far away for me to make out what they were. I knew them though. I'd heard them before.

"You know the words. You just have to say them."

I turned to find Grandpa standing behind me. "Do I?"

"Of course."

I nodded in agreement. Of course I knew the words. So why were they being so elusive?

A spinning top dropped to the long table in front of me. No, not a top. This was a spinning D12. I watched it for a long while though it never stopped spinning.

I was in the visitor's lounge at Grandpa's retirement home. The three TVs were buzzing static though no sound could be heard.

Grandpa looked at me with eyes more tired than usual. He smiled and glanced at the dice, still spinning.

It felt familiar, yet I couldn't place where.

"You know the words. You have but to say them." Grandpa repeated.

I heard it in my head again and recited it back, hearing it aloud. "This—this is a dream?"

"Of course it's a dream. What else would it be?" Grandpa moved one of the chess pieces and looked to me, awaiting my move.

I slid my queen to H4. "Checkmate."

"Well played, lad. But don't you have something more important to do than sit here playing games with an old man?"

"I think so. But I don't remember what."

A loud clap echoed on the table and a large book appeared in front of me. The arcanum Grandpa had given me. Droplets of blood fell from my forehead and landed on the cover. I'd seen this before.

"I remember this."

"Oh yeah? What happened?"

I tried to recall. It was all so hazy. The D12 continued to spin. "I think I bonded."

I watched the blood soak into the cover. The book opened to reveal red and black written pages just inside. The message that had been reserved for me was there, plainly visible.

"I don't know what it means."

My clothing shifted and I was wearing black robes. "Does this mean I'm evil?"

"Not at all. Good and evil are simply perceptions. Does the deer think the wolf evil because it must devour it? Does the bug think a car evil when it splatters on a windshield? No. Magic is a tool, used by many for any purpose. Some abuse it. Some praise it, and some fear it. Just because it can be used for evil does not make it inherently evil."

"But my robes—they're—they're black."

"So they are. What of it?"

"I thought black robes were worn by the bad guys."

"Have you learned nothing? It doesn't matter what color your robes are. It's how you use your power that matters. Your magic simply comes from a naturally darker place. You are a part of the balance that must be maintained, as are we all."

"What about Raj? He got sucked into a tornado because of me. And I killed Aleister. These black tendrils squeezed him and sucked the life out of him. I don't know how but I know I was controlling them."

"Aleister was a bad man who abused the powers he was given. Who's to say it was you who killed him. Remember when you sent that weak lightning bolt at me? Remember how it recoiled and shot back at you tenfold? When the magics are abused they tend to take their own vengeance. Even if it was your magics that ended his life, he was on a dangerous road that would have claimed him sooner or later. The best you can do is accept it and move on.

"As for your friend, I think I know someone who can help with that."

"Who?"

"You'll find her with an old associate, the same way you did before. But be cautious. She's crafty. And beware the toothy door."

"A rhyme, really?"

"Yes, really. You can't expect me to spell it out for you all the time."

I shook my head, wondering if this was really Grandpa or some aspect of myself that was taking his form.

"Oh, and in my study, provided it's still there, you'll find a set of horns on the wall. Be sure to take them with you. You never know when a good horn will come in handy. Now wake up."

My eyes shot open and I could hear sniffling somewhere nearby. I stirred and slowly sat up to find Mags sitting beside me, her face buried in her hands.

"Are you okay?"

She jumped and looked at me startled. "I thought you were dead!" She threw her arms around me and hugged tight. I have to admit I liked it.

"No, not dead. Not yet anyway. What happened?"

"I—I don't know. We were trapped and that guy was coming for us. Then Raj got sucked away and you started floating. Those robes appeared and then the next thing I knew both you and that guy, Alistair I think, dropped. He turned to dust and disappeared and you weren't breathing. Then the tornado just stopped."

I recalled most of the story but there were a few details I remembered differently. "Well, the good news, I think I know someone who can tell us where Raj is. The bad news, I can't guarantee they'll help us."

"Who?"

"I don't know for certain. I just have a hunch." I looked around the ruined study in search of the horns Grandpa had told me about. Sure enough, there was a set of three hollow steer horns arranged from smallest to largest hanging near the fireplace.

Picking myself up, I grabbed my arcanum and helped Mags to her feet.

We had to stepover, and sometimes climb toppled shelves, busted railing, and a wide assortment of debris, including hundreds of books that were scattered about the floor. I had a feeling Grandpa was going to throw a fit when he saw it, but then again I could just blame it on Aleister.

After what seemed like a journey to climb Mount Everest, I finally reached the fireplace. The flame had been extinguished and smoldering embers and ash were all that remained. I reached up and grabbed the bottom horn, the largest of the three.

"What do you need that for?"

"I don't know. Grandpa told me to take them. He said they'd come in useful." So I was paraphrasing. I didn't want to tell her my hunch was based on a dream that I couldn't prove was real.

I stretched a little further and dismounted the middle horn, using the length of the large horn to dislodge the smallest.

They were all three of identical shape, hollow on the large end with a small hole drilled into the smaller end. I nested them together and slung the group over my shoulder by a leather strap fixed to both ends of the large horn.

Opening my book, I found the page I needed. It came almost naturally, like the book knew what I wanted from little more than a thought. "Are you ready?"

"Ready for what?"

"To see if we can find Raj?"

"I guess. But if you're going to teleport, I thought those antitravel things stopped us."

I shook my head. I couldn't explain why but I knew this would work. I could feel the sigils all around the tower. They pulsed their energies, targeting something different than what I was doing. "I can do this. I have to do this."

"Okay." Mags stepped close and wrapped her arms around me. She pressed her soft lips against my cheek and kissed me. "For good luck."

I lifted the arcanum to hide my blushing face. For the first time ever, I felt like I was in control of something. I scanned the words inscribed into the obscure pages, recalling the last time I'd uttered them. Now that I understood their intent, I was amazed I survived the last time. This was literally the last thing I ever wanted to do but it was the only way I could think of to save Raj.

I felt the energies start to swirl around me. The wind picked up but nowhere near to the extend it had moments before. Lights flashed and all of a sudden Mags and I were standing at the edge of the forest trail in the dead of night with little more than a full moon to illuminate our way.

I didn't know why but I wasn't afraid any more. It felt more like whatever was in there was hoping I'd command it. That was wholly different from when I felt like it wanted to eat me.

"Are you sure about this?" Mags asked, clinging to my arm.

I found the sight somewhat amusing. She was dressed in golden full plate armor with a shield and warhammer at the ready, and here she was holding onto me, a thirteen-year-old kid dressed in black robes with a book in one hand and a set of horns slung over my back. We made quite the pair.

"Yeah. It's okay. There's only one thing in there that I can't feel. I'm willing to bet that's who we have to talk to." With a deep breath I walked through the tree line and let my eyes adjust to the lowlight.

It was much easier to see than I remembered. The contrast was more defined. Shades of blacks and grays were all around us but the grays helped to reflect the moonlight and illuminate the forest floor.

I picked my path and stepped onto a trail that cut to the right. We passed evergreens, maples, oaks, and just about every other assortment of tree I knew about, though most I had no hope of identifying in the lowlight.

I could feel eyes upon us, more curious as to our presence than anything but my fear remained absent. I'd changed. I was no longer the terrified little kid who'd struggled to even step into this forest a few hours prior. I was now something else— something darker. Sure, I was still a kid, a teenager even. But I'd learned some things. I was no longer defenseless. I could protect myself.

The path I was following curved around and I saw the sparse flickering lights I'd been searching for. We passed the thick row of evergreens that formed the perimeter outside the fence and I felt the ground go soft from pine needles.

"We're here. Try not to be scared. If anything happens, I'll teleport us out." I hoped I could still do that. I'd only done it twice now and both times I'd read it in the book. I hoped the concept was relatively the same for doing it the way Grandpa had.

The skull topped posts illuminated a short radius, revealing just enough detail to make out the bone fence, and of course there were now two absent their lanterns.

Off to the left there were three strange looking horses grazing in the foliage, though they didn't appear dangerous. If anything they looked more lean and swift than a standard horse.

At the center of the spectacle was the stilted house that looked like it was dancing on chicken legs.

"Hey, you, house. Look at me!"

"Aaron, what are you doing?" Mags whispered, trying to hide behind me.

"It turned to look at me last time. I don't want to be accused of trying to sneak. We're here for a purpose. I don't want anything getting in the way of—"

Before I could finish my words the cottage jumped and spun around. A narrow doorway faced me. It arched at the center and the top ridge pointed my direction as if inspecting us.

After a moment the door burst open. A large gangly woman with bony legs and arms, and a bulbous midsection stood in silhouette. Her face was elongated. A crooked and pointed nose angled awkwardly toward the ground. She stepped out the door and hobbled toward us. I could hear her whispering under her breath but I couldn't make out what she was saying.

She was mere steps away, highlighted in the lantern light when she stopped to survey us. "Fie, fie, that childish smell was never heard of nor caught sight of here, but it has come by itself?

Are you here of your own free will or by compulsion, my good youth?"

I couldn't help but notice the reflection of her teeth. I suspected they were made of some kind of metal. Behind her, an old-style broom swept tirelessly, removing her footsteps from the dirt.

"We come of our own free will, but compulsion carried us just the same. We seek a lost friend and I was told you might be able to help.

"See, see, I know not of lost companionship, for I'm but an old woman. But a price you may pay for my sightly eyes to seek."

"And what price is that?"

"Thrice the horns round thine neck. They were once mine when a tricky young lad flew away on the firebird's back."

"You want the horns?"

"Yes, yes." She pressed her gnarled fingers together and her disfigured tongue flickered with excitement.

"And if I give them to you, you'll tell us where our friend is?"

"Yes, yes. Give them to thee!"

"Okay."

"Aaron, wait." Mags whispered with urgency. "Make her deliver first. If she gets the horns there's no guarantee she'll tell us what we want to know."

"Clever little girl." The witch stepped forward and sniffed the air vigorously. "I've not tasted such a fresh morsel in so long."

I took a step back, shielding Mags from her. "You heard her. Tell us where our friend is first. Then I'll give you the horns."

"Thrice"

"Yes. All three."

"Very well. Follow thee." She turned and started back toward the dancing hut only to stop suddenly. "Would you get out of thy way!" The witch pushed the magical broom aside. It toppled over with a clap, only to pick itself up. No sooner than she passed, it immediately fell in behind her once again.

"Are you sure this is a good idea?" Mags whispered, keeping a wary eye not only on the witch but on everything around us. This was the stuff of fairytales and she didn't want to end up in the witch's oven.

"It's too late now. We have to see it through."

"I suppose you have a point there." Mags sighed.

A few steps from the hut, the witch stomped her scrawny foot and pressed her hands upon her wide hips. She cleared her throat as if demanding attention.

The hut stood with its back—did it have a back?—toward us. The doorway was nowhere to be seen.

Letting out an irritated bellow, the witch screamed into the night. "Turn your back to the forest, your front to me!"

The hut spun around to place its door for our entry, though it was in a different spot from where I'd seen it earlier.

A sly grin crept to my face. I knew I'd made the right choice.

The simple wooden door looked normal in all ways but one. It had a unique keyhole. I knew I'd seen it before. That fearful memory was what brought me back here.

Rather than a metal plate with tumblers, this keyhole was a wicked mouth full of jagged needlelike teeth. The clues from my dream fell into place.

The witch twisted the knob and the door came open with an eerie creak. She stepped aside and gestured for us to enter.

I was careful to squeeze past her. There was no trust in this relationship. It was a simple service. Information in exchange for the horns. If she tried anything else I was prepared to do to her what I'd done to Aleister, though I didn't want to think about it.

I waited for Mags to join me just inside the door before I continued deeper.

It was a simple hut, large enough for most, but the bulbous witch took up far more room that I felt was necessary. I had no doubt her lengthy arms could reach from one corner to the other, though there was no need to test it.

She was almost as tall as the ceiling and I found myself wondering why she didn't live some place with more room. The hut seemed a decent size from the outside, inside felt like a trap ready to spring.

"You give thine horns now, yes?"

"No! Not until you tell us where our friend is. He was pulled through a magical tornado and disappeared."

The witch cursed under her breath and hobbled over to a shallow basin resting atop an overturned crate. She snatched up a handful of clacking tiny slates that looked eerily of bone and tossed them into the air. Her pointed finger scratched inside the basin and she tossed a few more. On the third toss, a toothy smile stretched from drooping ear to drooping ear and she spun around to face us.

"I see thine companions, one blood and one bond. They slave in a house of stone. A place of reprieve. The sanctuary."

"Does that mean—"

"The council has them." I finished.

"Thy deed is done. Give us the horns!"

I started to take them off when I remembered I didn't have any idea how to get to Sanctuary. Something told me they weren't about to send another carriage. "How do we get there?" I asked, the horns raised but still very much secure.

"Not part of our deal, tricky boy. Give us the horns, we won't ask again."

"Do it, Aaron." Mags pleaded.

A quick look in her eyes told me she had some kind of plan brewing but I didn't know what. I sighed and released the horns.

The witch bounced with glee in a manner that should have been impossible for someone of her size.

"It's a shame you won't tell us how to get to Sanctuary. I'll bet we would have both happily done some chores in exchange for the directions."

"What? No, I don't wan—" Mags elbowed me in the ribs, silencing me.

The witch ended her joyful dance and raised an eyebrow toward Mags. "Thee would willingly perform chores?"

"Oh yes. We, the two of us, love doing chores." Mags shook her head in displeasure. "But since you won't tell us how to get to Sanctuary, I guess we'll just have to be on our way."

Mags started for the door, but the witch stepped into her path. The crooked nose seeped a slimy green substance as the witch nodded vigorously. She was mumbling something to herself, as if bargaining with some unseen force. "Yes, yes. I can take you to sanctuary. But *after* you do the chores." She raised a finger for emphasis.

"Okay. Where would you like us to start?"

The old crone glanced toward the ceiling and the tip of her nose nearly touched it. Her lips curled as she thought for a moment. "The stables. Yes, yes. The stables will do nicely. Clean the stables and work up a nice sweat. That'll bring out that childish smell."

Mags nodded her understanding and stepped around the witch to reach the door. I followed. It would have been stupid not to.

Once we were outside and clear of the witch's ear, I leaned in close. "Do you mind telling me what all that was about?"

"I think I know who she is. I remember reading about her. She has a near obsessive compulsion to make her visitors do chores in exchange for services."

"Who is she?"

"Baba something. It's been a long time since I read it. We have to be careful though. If I'm right, she's a trickster. We're going to have to outsmart her."

"And how are we supposed to do that?"

"Well, the last person who cleaned her stables stole one of her horses and got away. They're supposedly incredibly fast. And the horns you gave her—another traveler used them to escape on the back of some kind of bird."

"Firebird. She told me that when she saw the horns."

"That confirms it then. We need to find a way to escape, but only after she's told us where to go."

"Sounds easy enough."

I was wrong. It wasn't easy at all. I have no idea how long we worked making the stable good as new. My back was killing me from raking the soiled straw and laying fresh bedding.

Mags got the easy job of brushing all the horses down and cleaning their hooves. She informed me she used to spend the summer working at a stable and all of this was fairly simple labor. I didn't buy it. I suspected she was just telling me that to make me feel better.

I wiped the sweat from my forehead. I had no idea how anyone did any kind of work in such thick cloth. The robes were fairly comfortable all things considered but they didn't breathe very well and I was hot.

"Psst!" Mags signaled behind me.

I glanced the direction she was gesturing. All I saw was an old dirt covered tarp covering something on the back side of the wooden pens.

Mags continued brushing the last horse down as she worked her way toward me. "If that's what I think it is, it can take us to Sanctuary without her help."

"What do you think it is?"

She didn't respond. Instead, she made her way back toward the horse's head.

I heard a voice just outside the stables and saw the witch come into view.

"The children completed their task and another to ask. Yes, another to ask. You straighten the thistles before morning light, and then breakfast be within your sight." She commanded and disappeared the direction she'd come.

"I'm not straightening the thistles!" I declared just loud enough for Mags to hear. "I don't even know what a thistle is."

"I think it's a type of thorn."

"Why does she want us to straighten the thistles then?"

Mags shrugged. "I don't know. She's a trickster, remember. We need to leave now. I'm pretty sure she has a thing about eating children."

"You couldn't have said that part sooner?"

"You didn't ask."

I shook my head and stalked forward to make sure the witch wasn't outside. I caught glimpse just as she crossed the threshold and closed the door to her hut. Now was as good a time as any. "She just went inside."

"Let's go check it out." Mags laid the horse brush where she'd found it and slipped between two of the runs that had rotted away. She snatched her armor, weapon, and shield off the ground and quietly slung them over her shoulder. Unlike me, she was smart enough to remove the excess baggage before getting started.

We slipped closer to the ragged tarp and carefully pulled it aside. Underneath lay what looked to me like an extremely large stone bowl with an equally large wooden club inside.

"Please tell me that's not what you were hoping it was."

"Honestly, this is exactly what I was hoping for." Mags handed her armor and weapons to me and climbed over the lip, disappearing inside.

"What are you doing?" I asked as loud as I dared.

"Come on. Get in. We need to leave now."

I sighed and handed over her armor. She set it down inside the bowl and extended a hand to pull me up. In no time we were both inside the large bowl for reasons I didn't understand.

"This is a fantastic plan you had here."

"Shush. I just need to figure out how to operate it." Mags grabbed hold of the large club and rolled it toward her.

The bowl lifted off the ground and began to hover gently along the stable fence. "Yes! See, I told you I had a plan."

"I stand corrected. Get us out of here before she comes back."

Mags fiddled with the club and suddenly we were flying through the forest faster than I thought possible. Trees were whipping past and I could see a clearing just ahead.

A loud shriek echoed behind us and we both knew our escape had been discovered.

Mags pulled against the wooden club and we lifted higher. We were almost level with the clouds.

"What do we do now?" I asked.

"I guess we keep going until we get there."

"That sounds a little too philosophical, even for you."

Mags let out a soft chuckle. After everything that had happened, it was nice to see. "This is a mortar and pestle. The witch uses it to fly around and go places. I only remember it from one story, but the myth claims it will take you to the place of your heart's desire. Right now I desire to find Raj."

# Chapter 13
## Sacrilegium

A mixture of blue and orange scattered across the morning sky. We drifted through the clouds like a ship at sea, gracefully sailing across the silky vapors. From up here it didn't feel like we were moving fast at all but each time we broke the surface everything beneath was little more than a blur.

We'd traveled for what I guessed was about an hour before the strange vehicle began to slow and familiar sights came into view.

Mags was right. The mortar took us straight to Sanctuary in about the same time the carriage had. Of course, teleportation was much faster, but as Grandpa had said, it was forbidden, even if I knew how to get there.

We landed a few blocks away from the stone castle. I didn't have any idea what was going on inside and I didn't want to risk being swarmed the moment we touched down. I still didn't know how we were going to get inside. The guards were posted at the front door and I didn't know enough about this place to even consider another entrance.

I turned to Mags who was fastening the final piece of her armor into place. "Any ideas?"

She looked me up and down and glanced at herself. "Well, we could always try the infiltration approach. You look like a dark wizard and I look like a guard, though they're silver and carry halberds and I'm gold and have a hammer."

It wasn't a bad idea. We could possibly pass at a distance but I feared anyone who bothered to get close would immediately tell the difference. "Let's table that one for now and keep brainstorming."

We were both silent for a long moment before Mags nearly jumped with excitement.

"I've got one! But hear me out. It's kind of crazy."

"Okay?"

"Okay, so, you know magic, right?"

"Um, a little, I guess?" I found that a strange way to start the concept.

"I'm seeing a few ways we can play this but none of them are going to work. It's an impenetrable fortress full of people who want you, right?"

"I suppose."

"What if you surrender? You walk in and say 'Here I am', only when they take you it's not really you. It can be me, or better yet it can be an illusion. It creates a distraction that we can use to sneak in another route."

I thought about it for a moment and while it had some merit I didn't think it was a good idea to announce our presence, fake or not. And I wasn't about to let her go in there alone. "I still don't think we're there yet."

"Why don't you guys just take the crypt entrance?" A strangely familiar voice suggested from the alley beside us.

We both jumped. "Whoa, who are you?"

"Me? I'm nobody. Just someone who's been down on his luck for quite some time and happens to know a thing or two about that building you're thinking about sneakin' into."

"With all due respect, that doesn't sound like a nobody to me. That sounds like trouble." I hated the fact that we'd so carelessly been discussing our plans out in the open. Now we had another threat to deal with. Moreover, I couldn't shake the feeling like I'd seen this guy before. He felt familiar and foreign at the same time—like someone known but mysterious.

The figure shrugged. "Eh, do what you like. It's your funeral. All I'm sayin' is the crypt entrance is the only way in or out that doesn't have a constant guard. It empties into the old courtyard. Been off limits to students and faculty for years. Nobody goes there anymore, which makes it perfect for sneakin' around."

"I apologize, but I'm having a little difficulty believing you're a nobody with so much intimate knowledge about the place."

"I didn't say I was always a nobody. Bout thirty years ago I was the Archmagus of that school. Magehound assassins came in the dead of night. I barely got outta there in time. The next day my job was replaced by the council. I've been keepin' a close watch ever since. Don't get me wrong, the council's done a lot of good that I never had the stones for. But I knew somethin' like this would happen eventually."

"Something like what?" Mags asked, moving close in the hopes of seeing his face.

"The uprising. You can only keep a status quo for so long. Eventually someone's gonna learn how to play the system and take advantage of it."

"And why haven't you done anything about it?" I wasn't sure if I could trust this guy. It seemed a little convenient that he just happened to show up when we needed him to. But unexplained things had been my life lately. Maybe it was something in the magic trying to balance itself against all odds.

"I burned that bridge a long time ago. But if you want in that school, the crypts are the only way. I'll even show you the entrance if you'd like."

"I don't know if I can trust you." I said flatly, but it was Mags who surprised me.

"You can. He isn't lying."

"How do you know?"

She shook her head. "I don't know. I just—feel it. He's telling the truth."

I took a deep breath. I wouldn't have survived this night had it not been for Mags. I wasn't about to start doubting her now. If she said I could trust him, I'd listen. But that didn't mean I couldn't prepare for the worst. "Fine. Show us the entrance."

The sun was nearly risen when we arrived at the stone mausoleum. Our guide retrieved an iron keychain from beneath his stained overcoat and cycled through the keys until he found the one he was searching for. He inserted it in the lock and twisted. The iron grate creaked open.

"The tunnel's behind the third tomb on the left. It'll swing out. Once inside just keep goin' straight. It'll take you straight to an identical tomb on the other side. You're on your own from there."

"Thank you." Mags offered, though I remained silent. I'd give thanks once we were safely back on this side of the gate with Raj and Grandpa in tow.

We entered the mausoleum. Morning light filtered through stained glass on the upper walls. It took no time to locate the tomb he'd mentioned. It was on subtle hinges that were almost impossible to see. Upon studying it, it was remarkably similar to the surrounding tombs. I fiddled with a well hidden latch and the door swung out with ease.

It opened into a wide bricked tunnel with moss and cobwebs clinging to every surface. It was beyond dark in here but Mags' armor seemed to be glowing just enough to light our way. I was slightly unnerved by how relaxed I felt in here. Somehow beyond my comprehension I knew there were just over three thousand bodies buried nearby and I could feel each and every one of them. It was almost like they wanted me to give them a command but I couldn't bring myself to obey. It was too weird.

The tunnel went on for quite a distance. I guessed it had been built as an emergency escape in the event the castle had been breached. That was the only explanation I could see for its size. Seven or eight people could walk side by side without crowding.

As we walked I thought about the ex-headmaster—arch magus—whatever he was called. I couldn't shake the feeling like I'd seen him before. Suddenly it dawned on me. He was the old man I'd met at Grandpa's retirement home—Grigori. What was the old man doing here? Still, the fact that he carried the keys to this place was fortunate. I guessed the council had no knowledge of this tunnel's existence. I hoped so anyway. With a little luck maybe it would prove just as useful for our escape as it was for our infiltration.

We reached another door that opened into a small stone room with a sarcophagus at its center. A darkened stairway stood across the room. I could see beams of light peeking through the sealed doors.

Mags took the lead, pushing the right side door open.

I was taken back by how gloomy the courtyard felt. The grass and weeds hadn't completely overrun the place but it was far from kempt. There were statues everywhere. Some of powerful looking men. Others were odd winged creatures with animal faces, or sometimes a combination of creatures.

A stone fountain rested at the center of the courtyard. It had three tiers that had been dry for who knew how long. Hundreds of untouched coins from unknown eras and places rested beneath a thick layer of dust at the bottom.

Three sides of the courtyard were wreathed in towering walls and decorative columns that bridged the surrounding buildings. To my surprise there were no windows in sight. It was as if this place was a secret to the rest of the grounds.

Mags continued ahead, pausing at an iron gate that separated the quad from what appeared to be an old abandoned garden complete with hedge maze.

I hurried to catch up and suddenly I realized why she'd stopped. The gate was locked.

"I don't think I can squeeze through. You're pretty skinny. Can you try?" Mags asked.

I found the question silly. She was taller than I, but I had no doubt she could have gotten through. The only thing that would have stopped her was her armor.

"Probably, but I want to try something first." I grabbed hold of the ancient lock. It was rusted but appeared to be in relatively decent condition. I pulled the orange sparks around it and funneled them into the device. A moment later it clicked but the lock held fast.

I bit my bottom lip in frustration and released the lock. "It worked. I felt it work. Why didn't it open?"

Mags raised the flat side of her warhammer and gave a firm whack. The lock popped open. "Just needs a woman's touch." She smirked.

"And maybe a nice smack from a hammer?"

"You'd be surprised how many things a hammer can fix."

We opened the gate just enough to squeeze through and looped the lock back where it had been, though we didn't seal it.

Stepping into the hedge maze, we froze, realizing this was going to be more difficult than it looked.

"Which way?" I couldn't see anything other than walls of overgrown vegetation in every direction.

Mags studied our options for a moment before exhaling softly. She hesitated a moment and then pointed her hammer to the right. "That way."

We went right.

The sun had nearly crested the top of the foliage by the time we found the exit. For the first time since our arrival I could hear the sounds of movement. Something big was happening.

It sounded like a thousand-man army marching just on the other side of the wall. Only they were far from in-step, and far too spread out for any kind of formal march. Maybe a herd of cattle? I didn't recall cattle wearing shoes.

We ducked behind the nearest corner and waited for the shuffling of feet to pass.

It went on forever. Finally it became too much for me. I had to take a look and see what was happening. For all I knew a bunch of people were walking in circles, though I didn't think that was the case.

I crept forward and poked my head around the corner just enough to see what was happening. A freakishly long line of uniform wearing children were stacked three wide and who knew how many deep. They were being ushered by wizards in black robes to some place I could have cared less about. The tail of the line had to be back there—somewhere. It really didn't matter to me. I just wanted them to be on their way so I could get on with mine.

Mags leaned out beside me to take a look. "Where are they taking them?"

"I don't know but I don't remember things being this controlled when we were here last night. I'm guessing there's been a change of power. That's the only thing that makes sense."

"Do you think we should sneak into the line or wait for them to pass?"

"I think we should wait. It can't go on much longer, but then again I thought the same thing five minutes ago."

Eventually the line of children ended and we darted out into the open. The place was starting to look familiar now that the walls enclosed around us and the ceiling covered our heads. It was still a gargantuan castle but the presence of people meant common areas, and that meant we were close.

Mags took the lead, insisting she could feel which way we needed to go. I followed. She hadn't been wrong yet.

We found ourselves in a curved hall that seemed to be angling downward. I could feel something magical drawing near but I didn't know what could be so strong as to call to me like that. I suspected it was the same feeling Grandpa said I was giving to others, the thing I needed to control. I only hoped I'd figured that out by now. It would have sucked to come all this way just to have my enemies waiting for me.

The hall began to plane out and I could see light up ahead. There were three doorways along the right wall. Judging by the contour of the wall, that would place them on the inner part of the large circle we'd made.

Cautiously we neared the first opening and peaked around.

The room wasn't overly wide, maybe a twenty-foot radius. It had a simple stone floor and round walls. At the center a raised pedestal held a glowing object that looked a bit like an egg with unfurled flower petals.

I didn't care much about the strange object. It was the people shackled to the wall that caught my attention. Grandpa, Alice, the other two white wizards I'd seen during my hearing, and about five others I hadn't met were stretched by their wrists and chained to the ceiling. A wispy glowing smoke drifted gently from them and swirled into the top of the pulsing egg.

I could feel it pulling at me as well, but it was nothing compared to the colorful sparks it was draining from everyone else.

This had to be the arcane bank Grandpa told me about.

"Mags, will you smash that thing when I tell you to? And fair warning, it might explode."

"Okay." She took position over the top of it and readied her hammer.

I crossed the room to where Grandpa was held. His eyes were closed and his breathing was shallow. I stretched as close to the manacles as I could and directed the sparkling energies into them. It took a little longer than I preferred. The egg kept sucking the sparks from my spell but I finally managed to collect enough of them to envelop the iron bands. They clicked and popped open.

Grandpa's sudden weight fell onto me. It took every ounce of my strength to hold him up.

A voice echoed from the opening behind me and I nearly jumped in surprise.

"A-A-Ron, it took you long enough."

I turned to find Raj standing there. He still had on the gloves he'd taken from Grandpa's tower, but he was wearing the same uniform I'd seen the other kids wearing.

"Raj? What—what happened? Why are you dressed like that?"

Raj smiled. "It was awesome! I got sucked through that whirlwind with a couple other guys. We landed in an open field, but it didn't hurt as much as I thought it would. Anyway, I knew I couldn't let them see me or they'd use me against you, so I hid in the grass and waited to see what they'd do.

"One of them opened a portal. I knew that was my only chance to get back. Just as he was getting ready to go through, I used the gloves to pull his pants down and I jumped on his back. He tripped and fell into the grass and I dove through. The portal closed behind me. I realized pretty quick I was here so I stole some uniforms and slipped in among the other students.

"The black robes were leading us to some kind of assembly. I saw you guys in the hall and broke away to follow you here."

"Are you okay?"

"Yeah. I'm a little tired and a bit hungry but I'm okay."

"Do you think you can put your lockpicking skills to use and get these other people free?"

Raj glanced around the room at them. "Yeah."

"Okay. You start on that side. I'll start over here. Mags, once we have them all down, I want you to smash that thing."

"Got it."

I laid Grandpa against the wall and started directing energy into the collar around his neck. It took everything I had to keep my focus. It seemed every time a spark hit the metal band it dissolved.

"You can't—" A raspy voice whispered to my left.

I glanced up to see Alice, barely conscious and trying to talk to me. "What?"

"You can't open the collar with magic. It has to be done manually."

"Great." I turned to Raj who was moving slower than usual. He already had one of the white wizards released and was now working on the collar. "Raj, I'll handle the shackles. You focus on the collars. We have to get as many of these guys free as fast as possible."

"Okay."

In about ten minutes we had all of them down and their collars removed, though that part took longer than I liked.

"Mags, go for it."

She brought the hammer down on the egg-shaped orb and it exploded like glass. All kinds of magic released into the air. A fair amount found its way into the people around me but more went someplace else. I feared we were on limited time now.

"Come on. We need to move quickly. There's a secret passage we can use to escape but it's a bit of a walk."

We filed out and Mags took the lead since she was the one with the uncanny ability to choose the correct direction. I followed close behind her, ready for the moment when I'd have to react fast and hope I made the right decision.

Raj had taken position somewhere near the middle of our group, though I wasn't exactly sure where.

Two white wizards stayed behind me, carrying Grandpa. He still hadn't woken up. I was afraid I was too late to save him but they assured me he was still alive. I couldn't let myself be distracted by his state. Escape was our primary objective.

We made our way through the winding corridor and into the network of halls we'd taken to get here. To my surprise, we hadn't come across anyone. I hoped our escape would remain uncontested.

Finally, we came to an open ceiling where the gloomy morning light greeted us. I'd never been so happy to feel the cold air on my skin. We'd made it. All we had to do now was navigate the hedge maze and slip into the tunnels. Anything else could wait until we regained our strength.

As if my relief triggered it, alarms sounded and I could hear rushing footsteps not far off. Something inside told me they knew exactly where we were and there'd be no escape.

"Quick, this way!" I darted into the maze and hoped the others could follow quick enough to lose our pursuers. If we could reach the crypts before they found us we'd be in the clear. Those of us who could fight would have an ambush position, and those who couldn't would have an escape.

"There's a faster way!" Grandpa's voice reached me through the commotion. I spun to find him on his feet and squeezing through the others who'd bottlenecked. No sooner than he reached the head of our convoy, he extended his hand and began channeling. The vines, bushes, and branches that composed the towering flora walls began to unravel and separate. Within a few heartbeats' time we had an opening that traveled straight through the heart of the maze.

"Go!" Grandpa demanded, straining to hold the opening.

I let Mags and some of the others go first. Judging a good defense point, I rushed in after them, hearing a few of the others behind me. I guessed everyone was keeping up. Truth be told I wasn't sure. I could feel the vines closing in around us. The opening was getting smaller and I feared not everyone was going to be able to keep pace.

We ran with reckless abandon, squeezing through the constricting tunnel until we crossed through and found the iron gate blocking our path.

I glanced back and did a quick headcount. Everyone seemed to be present with Grandpa taking up the rear.

Mags fumbled with the disabled lock and pulled the gate open. She stepped aside, allowing the others to go first.

As soon as Grandpa and myself made it through Mags pulled it shut and slammed the lock into place.

We were home free. Just a little further and we'd be at the mausoleum and gone forever. Or so I thought.

# Chapter 14
## Acceptance

A deafening boom echoed behind me and I watched the ground split open. One of the white wizards fell into the gap, his screams echoed long after he disappeared into darkness.

My stomach churned. I didn't know such feats were possible and I feared Mags or Raj had fallen in.

I frantically searched my companions. To my relief they were clear of the opening, near a row of headstones. Grandpa was on the other side of the crack, helping one of the gray wizards who'd nearly fallen in.

The clouds darkened and several spots of orange started to appear. Before I knew what was happening flaming brimstone tore through and started to rain down upon us. The air was charged with electricity. A bolt of lightning crackled past me. I could feel my hair stand on end.

If I hadn't known about magic I would have thought we'd stumbled into the apocalypse. People were screaming and the temperature fluctuated rapidly. It was getting drastically colder but the energy and fire around us sent burning spikes through the area.

There was no telling how many were on our tail but judging from the noise I suspected a lot.

We ran for all we were worth. I feared it wasn't going to be enough. The only thing that could have made it worse would have been if archers had taken position on the walls surrounding us. We were in a kill box with one way out and we were nowhere near it.

I pumped my legs as fast as they would go, hoping to get just a little closer. I could see the mausoleum but it was still so far away. I had no idea how they swarmed us like they did. It was almost as if they knew where we were going. My mind came back to the archmagus. I couldn't help but feel he'd betrayed us.

I dodged an ice bolt and began wrapping my shield around myself. There was too much happening too fast and I was completely defenseless.

I heard the energy blast long before I felt it. It struck me in the back and I toppled face first into the overgrown grass. I could smell burning flesh and I suspected it was mine.

I wish I could say it hurt but I really couldn't feel it. It happened too fast to hurt.

My vision blurred and my hearing faded. It was like everyone around me was moving in slow motion. I was helpless but to witness everything happening around me.

I turned my head to find Mags. She was charging away from cover and headed straight for me. Someone grabbed her but I couldn't see who. She flailed and fought, trying to get free of their hold. The tears in her eyes told me things were worse than I thought.

If only I'd been able to feel, or understand, or to do anything really, I might have been able to comfort her.

Someone snatched me off the ground and I felt like I was floating. We bounced harmlessly across the courtyard, headed for the statues. I found that an odd choice. We needed to go to the crypts.

My body bounced off the ground like I'd been tossed roughly behind one of the strange winged creatures. I landed on my backside. Again, it wasn't so bad. I couldn't feel it. I was just glad to be able to see what was going on, though the horror of it made me wish I couldn't.

Bolts of energy shot through the air, firing this way and that. Bits of the sundered statues rained down upon us. Pretty lights flashed through the air.

I didn't know how many of our people remained. I could see at least four strewn about, their bodies twisted and mangled from the various debris and spells raining down upon us.

A pair of gloved hands grabbed the front of my robes and yanked me to the right. It was Raj. He was trying to tell me something but I couldn't hear. The silence had been replaced by a high pitched squeal that rang in my ears.

I wanted to tell him it was okay. That seemed like the right thing to do. He looked scared, though of what I didn't know.

I'm not sure when it happened but it was getting harder to breathe, like my chest wasn't moving the way it was supposed to. It made me want to be scared too, like Raj and Mags were, but I simply couldn't. I didn't remember how to be scared. I was just a head, floating above my body.

I remembered what Grandpa had told me about astral projection. It was like being in two places at once.

I looked behind me to find that thin green thread. Grabbing hold, I felt myself launch back into my body.

Sound snapped back to me and I could suddenly hear again. Dirt and bits of stone exploded all around. Bright flashes of light. Reds, blues, greens, yellows. They flashed passed as if we weren't even there. Figments in the chaos.

I squinted, trying to focus on the air around me. I could just barely make out the transparent shield and I realized I'd managed to erect it in time. I thought for sure the bolt that hit me had interrupted it.

"Raj."

"I'm here, A-A-Ron."

The tone of his voice confused me. It was almost like he was sad about something.

"Go protect Mags. I've got this."

He looked confused.

I watched his face for a moment, hoping he'd listen for a change. I didn't have time to argue with him.

Picking myself up, I turned to face the enemy. We were outnumbered almost ten to one. It seemed odd so many had come to collect me. Though I couldn't help but feel this wasn't about me. I was bonded now. I'd learned how to protect myself. Maybe this was something else entirely, something I just happen to be at the center of.

I looked over to where Mags was hunkered. Her face was covered in grit and sweat and tears but she looked mad as well. She had her warhammer gripped so tightly her knuckles were turning white. Her shield was extended over one of the wizards who'd been hit.

She peeked around a fallen statue and raised her hammer. The golden light exploded in a beam from the sky and sent one of the black robed wizards flying through the air. She ducked back just in time as a blast of red energy ricocheted where she'd been seconds before.

It made me smile. Even in all this chaos she was still the strongest person I knew.

My attention drifted across the field, inspecting the damage. Alice was lying face first in the churned dirt, refusing to move. A couple others appeared to share a similar fate, though they seemed to have made it a bit further than she. One of the gray wizards who'd been chained up was holding his left arm and I could tell there was no saving it.

Grandpa appeared to my right. He launched a volley of small yet powerful blasts that sent several of the attacking wizards running for cover. The few bolts that targeted him bounced harmlessly off his shield and imploded into nothing.

And here I was, standing at the center of the battle and not a single person seemed to notice me. I found that odd but stranger things had happened—stranger things like the thousands of dead calling to me. Even Alice was among them.

It seemed wrong to answer their call. I didn't know if I *could* ignore it. I didn't know if I *should* ignore it. We were drastically outnumbered and we needed all the help we could get.

Black tendrils outstretched from me and tethered themselves to the fallen. I was simply the vessel by which they rose. It wasn't just our people. A few of the black wizards rose too. The tendrils were trying to expand beyond my control and go into the crypts but I didn't let them. Those dead were already buried. I didn't want to risk waking them. But in total I had upwards of twenty servants ready to answer my call.

"Attack!" I shouted and the bodied began to climb to their feet. They were slow and a little clumsy at first but I expected they'd get back into the swing of things. I was always a little disoriented myself when I awoke in the mornings.

Movement caught my attention across the way and I saw two of the dark wizards sneaking up the back side of the wall behind Mags. What was worse, she was so focused on what was ahead of her she couldn't see them.

"Mags, look out!" My hand outstretched as if I could reach over and grab them. Somehow I did.

It wasn't the tendrils I'd come to expect but rather a pair of spectral hands. They latched onto her would-be attackers and drew the life out of them. Both were dead long before they hit the ground. To my surprise, I didn't feel the least bit bad about it.

Grandpa's voice rang out and I could hear him casting one of his vocal spells.

I turned just as he released and a swirl of energy rose into the sky. Lightning bolts danced from the clouds, striking here and there seemingly at random.

I twisted to avoid a wispy green substance that looked vaguely similar to a spider web. I instantly wished I hadn't.

As Grandpa was lowering his arms, it smacked him in the face and began wrapping itself around him. His shield didn't even attempt to block it which I found odd. What kind of magic could bypass a shield?

It tangled around his face and Grandpa struggled to get free. It seemed the harder he fought the more it engulfed him. I wanted to help I just didn't know how. I knew it was an enchantment but my experience with them was limited. How was I supposed to break a compulsion without a sudden shock to the system? I didn't even know what would shock him out of it. He was laid back about pretty much everything.

I took a moment to study the spell. It was a channeled effect which meant the caster had to be somewhere nearby. If I stopped him from channeling, the spell would end.

I turned and searched the field. My creations were spread near and far, engaged with the enemy. Most of the dark wizards appeared just as confused as the dead attacking them. I knew it couldn't be any of them. Even if they'd found some way to come to terms with my army, they were too distracted to cast.

I spotted a few of the more distant wizards flinging plasma bolts, fireballs, or the occasional lightning blasts but it couldn't have been them either. Like those before, they were otherwise engaged. Whoever had targeted Grandpa had to have a clear line of sight on him.

My eyes darted this way and that. Finally, I locked eyes with my target. A familiar gray wizard was cowering at the edge of the burning hedge maze. I recognized him immediately.

Eliphas was barely visible and he was chanting with a straight line of sight on Grandpa.

I nodded my approval, letting my emotions flow freely. I felt like a rabid dog ready to tear him apart. This was personal.

Eliphas may not have been the one to start all of this, but he certainly had a major role in it. Especially as far as I was concerned. And now he was fighting against us.

I couldn't let that stand. It was his altered vote that send us down this twisted and jarring path. I could have let that go. I could have even accepted that he was actively fighting against us. It was the fact that he was hiding like a coward and targeting my grandpa that got under my skin. For that, he would pay dearly!

I focused all my energy onto the squat cowardly man hiding in the weeds. I was going to hurt him, but that wasn't enough. I had to do more than just hurt him. I had to destroy him. I had to take away everything that would make him a person. Hurt him in the manner which would hurt the most.

My hands shook with rage as I reached for him. They sailed across the distance in the blink of an eye. He had line of sight on Grandpa. I had line of sight on him.

I could feel his life force waning against my necrotic touch. I wanted so desperately to rip him from his body and be done with it. That would have probably been kinder. But I wouldn't take his life. Not in the traditional sense anyway. In fact, I wanted him to live. The longer he lived, the worse his punishment would be.

I felt him struggle against my unseen grasp. He was helpless to escape. I already had him he just didn't know it yet.

My talons gouged out his eyes and shredded his tongue. His arms went limp as I ripped the tendons from his muscle and pealed the flesh from his face. It all happened so fast. Faster than he could comprehend. With a wave of my hand I'd rendered him disfigured, blind and dumb. He'd live the rest of his days in horror, able to hear the shrieks of those who beheld his monstrous visage.

Eliphas collapsed in a heap, unable to cry through the blood. He'd feel the pain of the damage he'd caused for the rest of his life. I'd destroyed everything that made him a person, everything that allowed him to connect to the world. It was all gone in the blink of an eye and he'd never experience it again.

I turned to check on Grandpa. He was still encased in the web but it was fading rapidly. In just a few moments he'd be free of it and back to his old self. Until then, he needed protection. I sent two of my newly risen creations to guard him until he regained his baring.

One by one the enemy wizards fell, only to be raised moments later. Each senseless death bolstered my ranks. In a matter of minutes the bloodbath had concluded. My friends were once again safe.

I glanced around to check on them. Mags was okay. I'd just checked on Grandpa. Raj was somewhere. I turned to find him and when I did I was shocked to see something I either hadn't noticed or had somehow forgotten.

My body was on the ground, a gaping hole burned through my chest. The skin around it was charred and blistered.

A realization came to me. If I was on the ground that meant I was in some other state. I looked around for the little green line tethering me. It was still in my hand, broken and unable to take me back to my body.

I heard Mags cry out as she ran for where I lay. She dropped to her knees and hugged me tight. I could see the tears free falling. They had that hint of gold in them she sometimes got.

And then I felt myself being sucked back into my body. The thin green line stretched toward its broken piece. I didn't have a choice but to obey. I was pulled like a dog on a leash.

My eyes slowly opened. I hurt so bad I could hardly move. My chest was pulling itself back together, filling me with painful breath.

"Aaron?" Grandpa knelt beside me and inspected the healing wound. "I'll be—that's some talent you've got there girly."

Mags didn't say anything. She was too busy holding onto me, which I didn't mind.

I waited for her to release before I tried to move. I hated myself for it but I knew I had to get up. My creations were getting restless and I needed to give them something to do before they caused any trouble.

"Sleep!" I commanded. To my surprise the army dropped where they stood, never to rise again.

I could feel the eyes on me and I knew from this day forward people were going to be scared of what I could do. But not my grandpa. He smiled wide and patted me on the shoulder. "I see you bonded."

"Yeah."

"Well, I can't say I know much of anything about your natural talents. We're on different paths. That limits what I'm able to teach you, but I've had a long career and I'm happy to teach you whatever I can. Just remember, a black robe doesn't dictate the kindness of your heart."

"Guys—" Raj called. "I've had about enough of this adventure. I'm ready to go home and sleep for a few days. Then I want to get back to our game and leave the real magic to the professionals."

# The End

# Author's Notes

I had a lot of firsts during the writing of this book. It was my first book after my grandpa's passing. My first project while running a YouTube channel. It was my first middle-grade targeted book. And my first first-person perspective. With so many firsts I found it difficult to stay focused.

I wrote this book in 30 days, doing a YouTube video log for each day. I wanted to show new writers it was possible to draft and write a story in such a short time.

And then it sat idle for almost a year until I finally decided to get it edited and published.

This book fought me every step of the way, from the initial writing to the editing. Even the cover. There wasn't a single aspect of this book that I didn't struggle with in one way or another. Now that it's finished I hope you enjoy the fruits of my labor.

As for the story concept, I went back and forth with my friend, George on what to write about. We tossed ideas back and forth until we settled on the concept of a kid visiting his grandfather at a home for retired witches and wizards.

I pulled the character concepts from a fair amount of figures throughout history. My main characters were based on the embodiment of character archetypes. Aaron is obviously a wizard. Mags was a paladin type. And Raj was a rogue, though being a book intended for a younger audience I wanted to portray him more as a prankster than a thief or assassin. This trio seemed to be a balanced way of including everything I might need without pulling in outside help or overpowering the characters in one way or another.

As for my side characters, Giles Corey was a man who was burned at the stake during the Salem Witch Trials.

Grigori Rasputin is a character which has popped up many times in popular culture for his unwillingness to die.

Aleister Crowley is another character who has been discussed at great length over the last century.

The witch in the woods was obviously the Baba Yaga.

And several other side characters were pulled by name if not by reputation.

I did this as a way of recycling historical characters into this world to add not only some history but some personality. My only regret, being this is such a short book, was that I didn't have the necessary room to evolve some of these characters further.

If this book is well received, I may see what I can do to expand it a bit further and see where Aaron's power takes him.

Once again, thank you for reading my book and if you got enjoyment from it, please take a few minutes to leave a review. Reviews help new readers find books and can make a major difference on the success or failure of a story.

Levi Samuel
December 2021